C[illegible]E ON VIEW

A perfect feel-good read from one of
Britain's best-loved authors

NICHOLAS RHEA

Constable Nick Mystery Book 33

JOFFE BOOKS

Revised edition 2022
Joffe Books, London
www.joffebooks.com

First published in Great Britain in 2007
by Robert Hale Limited

ISBN: 978-1-80405-114-6

CHAPTER ONE

When undertaking night patrols in towns and cities, constables were constantly reminded to walk along the inside edge of the pavements and as close to the buildings as possible. This was necessary, the sergeants explained, so that villains, ne'er-do-wells, drunks and other nefarious characters did not see us as we plodded silently and unseen in the shadows. It would enable us to catch them unawares and perhaps even surprise them in the act of committing an offence or crime. Catching someone actually in the act of perpetrating an offence always provided good evidence, but it was more important than that because it proved the arresting constable was doing his duty. It showed to the world and to his superiors that he was alert and very capable of fulfilling his responsibilities.

There is no doubt our dark uniforms made us almost invisible; indeed, our helmet and cap badges, in addition to the buttons on the uniforms we used for night patrols, were black instead of chromium plated which meant they did not glisten in the lights of houses, shops or passing vehicles. In modern times, when constables are depicted on television even in the daylight hours, they are often shown with black helmet badges—this is because chromium ones reflect the brilliance of camera lights when filming and so spoil the finished result. The actors must either wear dark badges or remove their helmets during filming. Authenticity is sometimes sacrificed for the sake of pictorial drama.

Theoretically, our instructions in the art of successful patrolling meant we could secretly observe the passing scene and, if necessary, be invisible during our approach to any troublemaker, shop breaker, burglar or inebriated reveller. We were almost like ghosts or shadows in the night. Many experienced constables would literally disappear in the darkness; they would stand motionless to watch events, or listen to the noises of the night without anyone realizing they were there. An added bonus of this well-developed ability to become invisible was that a constable could effect an arrest before the culprit realized he or she was nearby. It follows that many offenders experienced nasty surprises when constables suddenly materialized from the velvety darkness to clamp a heavy hand upon their shoulders. The shock and surprise was often sufficient to produce a spontaneous and voluntary admission of guilt.

The practice had merit. If an offender knew we were in the locality, he would leg it to safety or commit his crime beyond our view, consequently stealth during night patrols was considered a vital element in catching or outwitting rogues. In addition, one quick means of sobering-up an inebriated and happily singing, homeward-bound reveller was to call 'Good night' loudly from the shadows which often had the effect of causing him to break into a run to escape who or whatever was calling him in what he thought was a deserted street.

However, this ability to merge into the shadows could sometimes backfire. I recall one occasion when I was standing in the deep shadows of a corner in an alleyway, my back resting against a high stone wall as I enjoyed a brief respite from patrolling. The time was about 3 a.m. and my feet and legs were tired. All was quiet and Ashfordly was at peace; my position was made all the more pleasurable because a bitter east wind was blowing and my secret corner offered some small relief from its blast.

And then horror struck! Something fierce and nasty attacked me from above; a heavy weight landed on my peaked cap and knife-like claws dug into my face and neck as something shrieked and screamed. I shouted in alarm and terror and then in seconds it was all over. It was a cat. It had leapt off the wall above and behind me and landed directly on my head. I don't think it realized I was there. I'm not sure who received the greatest shock or surprise, but it ran off down the alley as I tried to regain my breath and calm my nerves.

On another occasion I was on night patrol in Strensford, walking along a deserted street which, in the daytime, was constantly busy with shoppers. The entire street was known locally for the variety and quality of its shops and cafés and our job, on night duty, was to check the rear entrances and windows to all the premises, making sure none had been attacked.

The rear parts of some shops were extremely vulnerable to thieves who broke into premises under the cover of darkness; quite often no one was living nearby to hear them and raise the alarm. Access to those rear doors and windows was often through a long and narrow dark alley and on this occasion, I was plodding up the street shaking hands with the knobs of doors which fronted the main street. After checking the front of the premises, therefore, I had to go down one of those dark alleys to visit the rear. I was extremely tired and almost asleep on my feet and, as I turned down an alley, my torch lighting my way, I was shocked and terrified to see someone standing there, looking directly at me. It took a few seconds to realize it was my own reflection in a polished black marble panel which bordered a large shop window. I had mistaken the panel for the tunnel-like entrance to an alley. It goes without saying that the experience jerked me into full wakefulness.

Our night patrols, usually in urban areas rather than the countryside, meant we had to conceal ourselves for most of the time, unless, of course, there was need to show the uniform. Making our presence obvious to everyone would be necessary, for example, outside a dance hall or pub, or perhaps other places where noisy youths congregated, or trouble was likely to occur, particularly during the night-time hours. On most occasions the mere presence of a solitary uniformed constable on duty ensured good behaviour—such was the respect afforded to the office of constable.

During daylight hours, however, we adopted a completely different strategy for our routine beat patrols. Under normal circumstances, we had to ensure we were always on view and we had to perform our duties in such a way that the great British public and indeed any overseas visitors could see us. This meant we must always be smartly dressed with brushed uniforms, well-pressed trousers, shining boots and neat haircuts while never doing silly things like eating ice-creams or smoking cigarettes on the street or in public places while in uniform.

A constable's smart appearance had the effect of deterring petty crime and trouble-making but it also provided a welcome assurance for those using the streets or public places. The sight of a lone constable in uniform standing in a prominent position was undoubtedly considered important in maintaining the Queen's Peace and, when foreign visitors came to our shores, they would often ask if they could photograph us. They loved to see the traditional British bobby on patrol, particularly as we did not carry firearms in the manner of many other police forces. Indeed, the entire system of beat patrols was arranged so constables were constantly on view to the public. In addition to the assurance this created, it also meant they were instantly available when required whether it was for something simple like reporting a lost watch or wallet, sorting out a traffic jam or even performing urgent first aid on an injured person. Patrolling constables might also have to deal with something infinitely more serious such as a traffic accident, wounding offence, or even murder.

I knew one rookie constable who had to deal with a traffic accident involving a collision between a carful of

Chinese and another full of Italians, none of whom spoke English, while another had to cope with a suspected murder within twenty minutes of beginning his very first beat patrol. That the incident was later reduced to manslaughter did not detract from its seriousness—a group of celebrating workers threw a colleague into the river as part of some bizarre initiation ceremony, but the man could not swim. He drowned before their very eyes, even as that young constable was running to the scene.

Such a baptism of fire highlights the responsibilities and the variety of demands that are placed upon a patrolling police officer. It also shows that the moment a constable dons the uniform, members of the public assume he or she is fully trained, widely experienced and capable of expertly performing any of his multifarious duties. Furthermore, it illustrates why police work is never boring; quite literally, the constable on patrol never knows what lies in wait around the next corner but whatever it is, he must deal with it confidently and efficiently, often in the full glare of public scrutiny. Even if constables lurk in the shadows, most of their work is done in full view of the public.

Having said that good constables are always on view when necessary, I should perhaps qualify that by highlighting a piece of police lore which says, 'A good constable never gets wet'. This reinforces the old saying that rules are for the obedience of fools and the guidance of wise people. A good constable will always be on view, but the possibility of getting cold and wet might require him to exercise some necessary discretion.

The notion that a constable should be constantly visible during the day and at other necessary times could be echoed in the fact that the views on the North York Moors and indeed in some parts of the Yorkshire Dales are also virtually limitless, ending only at the horizon where they disappear into infinity. Because much of the very high ground does not encourage the growth of trees such vistas are plentiful and stunning. Bleak and windswept heights overlook thousands of acres (or hectares) of unbroken heather and bracken, the panorama being interrupted only by scattered dry stone walls, isolated shelters or lonely farmsteads. It means that the folk of the Yorkshire uplands are accustomed to enjoying long-distance views.

There is a lovely story of an upland farmer from the moors retiring after his wife had died and, because he had never travelled overseas, his children treated him to a holiday in the Swiss Alps. On the second night, his son rang the hotel to see how he was enjoying himself and asked, 'Is there a good view from your hotel bedroom?' The old man replied, 'There would be, if it wasn't for all these mountains.'

A constable wishing to see what is happening in the distance can do worse than position himself on one of those lofty places around the dales and moors so that he can survey the scene far below. A pair of powerful binoculars or a telescope is an undoubted asset, but one must realize that if you stand upon an elevated site, then you also are visible to those below. A constable silhouetted on the skyline is as obvious as a lonely tree, factory chimney, standing stone or parish boundary way-marker. He can be seen from miles around, so the secret is to shield oneself with something like a copse of trees, a barn or high wall.

The moors around Aidensfield are typical of those elsewhere within the North York Moors National Park. Thick with heather that produces a wonderful purple carpet in mid-August, the loftier areas are virtually devoid of trees and shrubs. Constantly swept by the wind, even on quiet days, the slightest breeze rustles among the heather and stirs the grouse, peewits and skylarks into activity. The wind sighing through the heather, even on the calmest of days, is one of the sounds of peace on those moors. If a tree does succeed in growing, it will usually be a rowan or hawthorn which, in maturity, slopes to the east because the prevailing winds generally come from the west. I've known tourists ask why the few trees which survive on the heights always lean over—that is the reason; they have not been struck by passing buses, lorries or low-flying aircraft.

The moorland heights are divided by deep valleys whose bases are far below the peaks. These are the dales, so lush and green. With flowing rivers or becks, extensive fields, woodlands and small stone villages, they provide a haven from the surrounding wild and harsh territory.

Looking into the dales from high viewpoints, it is possible to see people moving about, cars going about their business, trains moving like snakes along winding lines, smoke rising from domestic chimneys, children playing at school, animals in the fields, fishermen sitting quietly by the water, farmers busy with their seasonal work and, at weekends, visitors wandering along moorland paths or beside the meandering rivers.

There are the sounds too—when standing on an elevated patch of ground, it is possible to hear the sounds which rise from the dales and villages, some being lost among a general hum of other noise and others sounding clear and bell-like. At times it is possible to overhear, from far below, the conversations of villagers, the sound of radios, the hum of farm machinery or the engines of cars and lorries struggling up some of the inclines. I find it quite puzzling that sounds, like the smoke of bonfires and house fires, should rise heavenwards in this way. It is little wonder that artists, musicians and writers come to these moors for inspiration—quite literally, each of those viewpoints provides a wonderful microcosm of country life as a whole, or perhaps merely a window upon an isolated or particular village community.

It was while standing upon one of those elevated stretches of moorland, something in the region of a thousand feet above sea-level, that I noticed a woman hurrying along the street in the tiny community of Gelderslack. It was a late September day with bright sunshine and clear views, even if there was a distinct autumnal chill in the air.

From the distance, she looked like a Lilliputian character in her red coat, but even from that distance, I recognized her. Her name was Jenny Stanwick. Mrs Jenny Stanwick in her red coat was a familiar sight to those of us who lived in the area. For a few minutes, I watched her progress and noted the service bus crawling down a steep incline towards her; naturally, I thought she was heading for the bus stop. This was confirmed when she disappeared from my sight as she hurried behind the chapel and a line of conifers that adjoined it. The bus stop was near the chapel. I thought no more of the incident until her husband came to my police house the following morning and said, 'Mr Rhea, summat funny's happened: our Jenny's vanished.'

CHAPTER TWO

Alan Stanwick arrived at the police house just before eight o'clock. We were out of bed, trying to get the children ready for school and persuading them to eat their breakfasts. There were the usual scenes of juvenile bedlam in the tiny kitchen, but the hammering on the door demanded my attention so I left Mary to deal with our domestic matters.

'Now then Mr Rhea.' Alan worked for Maddleskirk Abbey Estate, helping with the maintenance of the complex heating system in the abbey church and its monastery. His plumbing expertise was of immense value; having updated an older system he was familiar with every part of the network of pipes and valves. The abbey with its complement of about 120 monks was about two miles away from Aidensfield and although it was not on my beat, being the responsibility of my neighbouring constable, I found myself covering it whenever he was away on leave or a day off. Alan, however, lived in my patch so it was logical he should come to me if he needed a policeman. His home was an isolated smallholding at Gelderslack deep in the moors; there he kept a few pigs, sheep, hens and turkeys that helped to supplement his income. He was around forty-five, tall and broad-shouldered with thinning light-brown hair and a pleasant manner. I believe he had worked for the abbey all his life.

'Morning, Alan,' I greeted him, wondering what on earth he wanted at this time of day.

My first thought was that he'd been involved in a motoring accident on his way to work, or he'd witnessed something I should know about.

'Something wrong?'

'Aye there is, Mr Rhea,' and that's when he told me his wife had vanished. There was a look of uncertainty on his face as he told me his story, and more than a hint of misery and unhappiness as he wrung his cap with his hands.

'Vanished? Look, you'd better come into the office. Would you like a cup of tea?'

'Aye, that would be nice, I've been out since sun-up trying to find her, I came without my breakfast. . . .'

'We might rustle up a fried egg, some bacon and a sausage or two.' I was thinking of Mary's battle to persuade our children to eat everything she had cooked. There was bound to be something spare and I'd rather Alan ate it than have it thrown into the dustbin. He looked as if he needed something to cheer him up.

'Lovely, but look, Mr Rhea, I didn't come here to be a nuisance, it's just that I don't know what to do. Mebbe I'm making a fuss about nowt, but I thought I'd call in on my way to work, just for chat.'

'You did the right thing so come into my office; I'll get Mary to fix something to eat and then we can talk.'

I seated him at one end of my desk in the office, away from the family noises in the kitchen. I sat at the other, notepad at the ready.

I closed the door between the office and house in an effort to maintain his confidentiality and for the first few moments, we chatted about nothing in particular. I wanted him to be settled before I began my questions; I hoped his misery would not prevent him telling the full story.

Within minutes, Mary arrived with a tray bearing a plate of hot breakfast, some slices of toast and a jar of marmalade all accompanied by a big mug of tea. I'd already finished my breakfast but accepted a mug of tea so that I could keep him company as he enjoyed his breakfast.

'So, Alan, tell me what's happened.'

I could see he was famished because he tucked into the sausage before he began his tale, savouring it as he took a mouthful of fried egg and a forkful of bacon.

'By gum, this is grand,' he said with a weak smile. 'I've had nowt since last night except a pork pie and pickled egg in t'pub. I might have got summat at work this morning but would have had to wait till dinner-time. The monks have their breakfasts about seven and dinner about twelve thirty . . . we can allus get summat from t'kitchen. Anyroad, I appreciate this, I really do. Not what you'd expect when you go to t'police.'

'It's the least I can do, Alan. Now, down to business. You say Jenny's disappeared?'

'Aye, I can't fathom it at all, Mr Rhea. Just upped and gone with never a word. It's not like her, not like her at all.'

'She's not left a note?'

'Nay; I've looked everywhere. And all her stuff's still in t' bathroom and t'bedroom. Make-up, toothbrush and so on. Best clothes and whatever. She's only got what she went out in, but she's taken her handbag. I've no idea whether she has any money in it. If she has, it won't be much, not enough to get her very far. Mebbe a local bus fare and a bit for shopping.'

It was his reference to the bus that made me recall seeing her the previous day. 'I saw her yesterday, Alan. I was up on the moor and happened to be looking down on Gelderslack. I'm sure it was Jenny, a lady in a red coat. I saw her passing the chapel just as the bus was coming in.'

'What time would that be?' He was still tucking into the breakfast.

'Yesterday morning, about eleven or so. I must admit I didn't check the exact time.'

'Aye, well, there is a bus about eleven, it goes to Ashfordly and then onto Eltering. She sometimes catches it when she wants to go shopping in town. So did she have owt with her? Suitcase mebbe?'

'I can't remember noticing she was carrying anything. She was just hurrying along the village in that red coat, and she was alone.'

'Aye, well, she wears that coat when she's going off somewhere; she likes to be smart when she's out of the house and away from home.'

'So it looks as if she was intending to leave Gelderslack. On the bus perhaps? Where have you checked?'

'Well, I was out last night, our regular Tuesday darts match at t'Black Lion in Shelvingby and got in about eleven. She wasn't in when I got home from work just after five but I thought nowt of it. She does go out quite a lot and with me going off to play darts that evening, she'd no need to bother fettling my supper because t'pub would put summat on for us. They allus feed t'darts teams. Anyroad, I saw to t'animals and things and then got washed, shaved and changed and went off to t'match in my car. I do it every Tuesday, Mr Rhea, regular as clockwork, and she goes off somewhere, meeting friends, shopping or whatever. On t'bus.'

'And you are sure there was no message from her? A note left somewhere?'

'No, nowt.'

'Did she ring you? You've the telephone in, haven't you?'

'Aye, but I was out, you see. Feeding up straight after work, getting washed and shaved upstairs, going out to t' match . . . mebbe somebody did ring, but I never heard 'em. She'd know my routine, though, she'd know not to ring when I was out and about. She'd pick her time.'

'So have you any idea where she might be?'

'Well, when she wasn't in when I got home from work, I thought she must have gone to see her mother or done a bit of shopping, and she'd be catching the last bus. That would have got her home about nine o'clock. As I said before, there was nowt unusual in that, not on darts night. Anyroad, when I got in after darts and realized she wasn't there, I thought summat must have happened at her mother's, making her stay over to see to the old lady.'

'Is she alone? Her mother?'

'Aye, she was widowed a few years back. She manages most of the time, but likes help with the heavy stuff, like washing t'sheets and ironing, so Jenny goes to help out. She hasn't the phone in, her mother I mean, so when I rang her mother's neighbour this morning to ask her to check at her mum's, Jenny had never been there. The neighbour went round to check for me—we can ring her if we want messages passing on.'

'So where does Jenny's mother live?'

'Ashfordly. On that big council estate near t'graveyard. Ash Tree Road. Number 17, Mrs Crompton.'

'So when was the last time she saw Jenny?'

'Last week, Tuesday I think. Jenny pops in most Tuesdays when she's not seeing friends or going shopping.'

'Are you worried about her?'

'Well, I wasn't, not last night. Puzzled more like, Mr Rhea. I mean, she does go off a lot on her own because I'm out at work all day and like I said she often stays out later if I've a darts match on. She uses the bus because I take the car to work, or sometimes she might get a lift from a neighbour. I didn't sleep last night, wondering if summat nasty had happened to her and I must admit I got a bit worried when she didn't turn up by this morning. She would know where I was, so she could have rung late, when I'd got home from the pub. I'd have heard the phone then, even if I was in bed.'

'The phone's downstairs, is it? You've not got an extension in the bedroom?'

'No, never felt t'need for that sort of thing. Telephones in bedrooms! Whatever next! But with her not turning up or ringing, I wondered if she'd missed t'last bus and set off to walk home . . . I checked this morning, on my way here. Looked in ditches and hedge bottoms, in case she'd got knocked down or summat, but there was no sign of her.'

'You've asked your neighbours?'

'Aye, not that we've many where we live, most are a long way from our house but those I asked never saw her yesterday or last night. I got round most of 'em this morning. You say you saw her getting on t'bus?'

'Not exactly getting onto it, Alan, but I saw a lady in a red coat heading towards the chapel, where the bus stop is. And the bus was heading into the village at the same time. As I said, I thought it was Jenny; I do know her by sight but I was quite a long way from her.'

'It wouldn't be anybody else, Mr Rhea, not in that red coat and not in that part of the world. Gelderslack's not exactly throbbing with life.'

He was right. It was the tiniest of hamlets in a remote setting with nothing but half-a-dozen houses and a chapel. No high street, no shop, no inn, no village hall and not even a village centre. Just those few houses and farms scattered around the moor at both sides of a narrow little-used road.

'Have you had a row of any kind? I have to ask this. Anything that would make her want go off to be alone?'

'Nay, Mr Rhea, me and Jenny never fight or raise our voices. We get on right well, allus have done even though we've not managed to have a family. We keep ourselves to ourselves, look after t'animals and mebbe go out at weekends, to t'pictures or for a bar snack or summat. Best of friends we are. I've never known her raise her voice or grumble about things. Me neither; I'm not one for complaining or making a fuss. We're as happy as pigs in muck, both of us.'

'Has she been ill recently? Depressed? Worried about something?'

'Not so far as I know, Mr Rhea. She's never ill and she's never said she was bothered about anything, and we've enough money to get by. We're not rich, but we've enough for the two of us. I think she would tell me if she was really upset or worried about summat. I don't think she's ever been to see a doctor, if that's what you're getting at. She'd have to catch t'bus to Ashfordly if she wanted a doctor, or he'd have to come out here to see us, we've none anywhere near us.'

'And if she did find herself having to stay away overnight for any reason, she'd ring you? You're sure about that?'

'Aye, she would. We allus keep in touch if one of us is going to be late home. That's why we had t'phone put in.'

'When you rang her mum's neighbour this morning, did you ring anywhere else? The hospital for example? Jenny's friends? Anywhere she might have gone?'

'Nay; I thought she'd ring me if she was in bother of any kind, or if summat had happened. And she would, she's good like that. If she'd had an accident and gone into hospital, they'd have rung me, wouldn't they? I mean, I could have been ringing all over t'spot, not knowing where she might be, causing panic and upset. Like I said, I'm not one for making a fuss about things, Mr Rhea, I didn't want folks upset if it was all over nowt.'

Alan's problem put me in something of a dilemma because it was not the task of the police to go seeking adults who had left home voluntarily. It was always accepted that an adult person could leave home at any time and for any reason; it did not matter that they abandoned a partner, spouse or family or if they disappeared without giving any kind of explanation. If a family did wish to try and trace an absent member, there were agencies to help them, such as the Salvation Army.

Quite simply, it was not the duty of the police to get involved in that kind of domestic drama unless, of course, the circumstances suggested something sinister or suspicious. If the missing person was physically ill or mentally impaired, for example, then we would make the necessary enquiries, just as we would if it was suspected he or she was a victim of crime or the perpetrator of a crime.

Likewise, if we thought the missing person's life was in danger we would make a search. Clearly, we would also do our best to find a bewildered old person who had wandered away, and we would always hunt for missing children and young people, or even ramblers who got lost or overdue during walks on our moors.

In short, our action depended upon the prevailing circumstances, but I did not think my superiors would sanction an immediate search for Jenny Stanwick, harrowing though it was for Alan. Nonetheless, I was mindful of the fact she had not taken her overnight things such as make-up and a toothbrush, nor had she left a note—that suggested she had not intended staying away from home and so there would have to be some careful consideration of the circumstances. Maybe there was something suspicious about her disappearance? Something I had not yet noticed? Maybe I would have to dig a little deeper into his version of the event. If I became sufficiently suspicious about her disappearance, then I would have to search the family house for any kind of evidence or leads. I had no desire to upset Alan by doing that at this early stage; at the moment, I had no evidence of anything suspicious.

Despite the well-documented official uninterest in adults who voluntarily leave home, those of us on patrol in the vicinity of Ashfordly, Eltering and district could keep our ears and eyes open for Jenny. I would issue a localized circulation to all our patrols; it would be our unofficial contribution to his welfare.

I explained the procedures to Alan and he nodded his understanding. I could bend the rules a little further by undertaking more than a mere watching brief and promised I would do something positive to help. I would begin by visiting Jenny's mother in Ashfordly during my routine patrol today and then I would make general enquiries in the district. If she had not turned up by this evening, then we might consider listing her as 'Missing From Home' on our circulars, although no special hunt would be launched.

That might occur if other factors came to light, such as suspicion of a crime either by her or against her, or a possible mental breakdown. One reason for listing her as 'Missing from Home' would be in case a woman's body was found somewhere, or perhaps if someone matching her description was admitted to hospital with a loss of memory or lack of identification documents after a bad accident. Her name on an official list could help in the search for such a person's identity.

While Alan was sitting in my office, however, I rang Ashfordly District Hospital and St Aidan's Hospital in Elsinby just to check, but she had not been admitted to either of them nor had she been treated there for any injury. Then I rang Eltering Police Station, our sub-divisional office, to check whether Mrs Jennifer Stanwick had been involved in any kind of event which necessitated either detention in a police station or admission to a specialist hospital, say at Leeds, Middlesbrough or Scarborough.

I provided a brief physical description for I knew her well enough to provide that. There was no record of her, neither was there a record of a woman of her age and description being admitted suffering from loss of memory.

I told him, 'When I'm out on patrol, Alan, I'll check with the bus service to see if the driver remembers Jenny boarding his vehicle yesterday and if so, where she alighted. He should remember that red coat. Now, what about her friends? The people she visits or goes shopping with? Who are they? I'll need to talk to them.'

'I don't know where they live or even their surnames, Mr Rhea. She's never told me—she just says she's off for a day's shopping with Sylvia or lunch out with Marie and Sue, or popping in for a chat with Brenda. . . . I've met some of 'em, but I don't know their surnames or where they live.'

'Fair enough. I'll see if her mum knows when I talk to her. In the meantime, I think you should go to work now; that's where she'll ring if she wants to get in touch during today, and if you hear any news can you ring me? Either Mary will take a message here, or you could contact either Ashfordly or Eltering Police Stations. I'll make sure they know about this.'

Having done what he could, Alan prepared to leave for work, but before he left, I asked him to ring his home, just as a final check in case Jenny had returned since he'd left for work. She hadn't; he got no reply.

When he left, and before going out on patrol, I completed the necessary paperwork which resulted from Jenny's disappearance, then made my way to Ashfordly Police Station to ensure the incident was made known to all local patrols, including those operating from Eltering and Malton. Fortunately, Alf Ventress was on office duty in Ashfordly Police Station and, knowing the Stanwick family quite well, said he would do what he could to trace Jenny while I completed my entry in the occurrence book. As I worked on my entry, which was a form of diary kept to record every incident, large or small, which effected the operational functions of Ashfordly Police Station, Alf began to make some phone calls.

Although I had rung both Ashfordly and Elsinby Hospitals, he decided to ring them again and include Eltering Memorial Hospital on his list, just in case Jenny had been admitted or treated since my earlier call. That was typical of Alf—he wanted to satisfy his own curiosity by checking and rechecking every possible avenue of enquiry. When I had completed my book entry, I turned to him.

'Anything?'

'Nothing so far,' he said ruefully. 'The only emergency at Ashfordly General was a painter who fell off his ladder yesterday morning. He broke his arm and smashed a cheekbone. He's been kept in because he had a nasty bang on the head. They thought he might have fractured his skull, so he's being kept in till they know for certain. It might just be concussion. Apart from that, they said it's been the quietest night for years. Look, Nick, you go about your enquiries, leave the phone calls to me. I'll spread the word. The sergeant's not in today, so he can't check on us and ask what we're doing. We needn't worry about spending police time on this one and there's nothing else spoiling, nothing needing our immediate attention. It's the least we can do for Alan; he's a decent chap and I can guess how he's feeling right now.'

My first call was upon Jenny's mother. I made my way to the council estate with its bow-shaped road of smart houses built of local stone—a prize-winning development at the time of its construction—and I easily located No. 17.

I rapped on the letter box and after a short delay, the door was opened by a lady whom I guessed was in her late sixties. She wore a floral pinny and was wiping her hands with a towel—clearly, she was in the midst of baking something.

'Mrs Crompton?'

'Yes?' I could see the look of concern that crossed her face at the sight of a policeman on her doorstep. Usually, such a presence heralded bad news and to be honest my news was not good.

'I'm PC Rhea from Aidensfield,' I introduced myself. 'I wonder if I might have a word with you? Inside?'

'Oh, yes, sorry, I should have asked you in . . . it was such a shock, seeing you there . . . do come in, Mr Rhea.'

She led me into her small but neat living-room and bade me be seated in one of the armchairs near the fireplace; the fire was not lit. She settled in the chair opposite, a worried expression on her face as she waited for me to explain.

'I don't want to alarm you,' I began, as if my words would make any difference. 'I had a visit this morning, from Jenny's husband.'

'Alan?'

'Yes, he called at my police house on his way to work.'

'Oh.'

I paused before continuing, wanting her to realize I had something serious to tell her.

'He's worried about Jenny; she didn't come home last night and he's had no message from her. Now, Mrs Crompton, we've no reason yet to be unduly concerned about her absence, but I am trying to ascertain whether you can help—for example, did she visit you yesterday? Or have you any idea where she might be? Do you know her friends?'

'Oh dear, that is unusual. Our Jenny? Not come home? It's not like her, Mr Rhea, she always lets us know where she's going and how long she'll be . . . and I don't think she's ever spent a night away from home without Alan . . . they're very close, you know, very close.'

'That's what he suggests. Now, he says she often comes to visit you.'

'She does, very regularly on Tuesdays, it's Alan's night out, he goes playing darts—he's in the team—but not yesterday. She told me she wouldn't be coming this week; she does miss the odd week now and again.'

'So you never saw her at all yesterday? Not even for a quick visit?'

'No, but I'm expecting her next Tuesday.'

'So where might she go, if she didn't come here? I think she caught the bus from Gelderslack yesterday morning at eleven and it comes here to Ashfordly, then continues on to Eltering, going through all the villages.'

'That's the one she gets when she comes to see me, Mr Rhea. It's the only one on a morning anyway so she hasn't much choice. She catches that one when she goes out for the day, seeing me or going shopping or whatever. And if she stays late, she catches the last bus back home.'

'So where might she go if she didn't come here?'

'She might go shopping in Ashfordly or Eltering by herself, or mebbe visit a friend, or even go shopping with a friend in those places. Have dinner out too, or just a snack. Make a day of it. You don't think she's come to any harm, do you? This is most unlike her, most unlike her.'

'I must stress we've no reason to be concerned for her safety, Mrs Crompton, not at the moment but clearly, the longer she is away without contacting Alan, the more concerned we're all going to get. I need to know the places she's likely to visit, and the people she might be seeing. Alan doesn't know.'

'Well, they're her friends, not his. He's got his mates in the darts team and cricket team, and she's got her old schoolfriends. She does most of her shopping here in Ashfordly, the weekly stuff that is, but she wouldn't stay overnight, would she? Even if she'd gone to see a friend and missed the last bus home, she'd let Alan know; they had the phone put in, you know. Do you think she's been hurt, Mr

Rhea? Is she in hospital? Unconscious maybe? Unable to give her name?'

'We've checked all the local hospitals and my colleagues at the police station are doing a second check, just to be sure. If she has been admitted, whether her name is known or not, we'll be informed.'

'Oh dear; I do hope she's not lying hurt somewhere . . . I mean, Mr Rhea, suppose she missed the last bus home and started to walk, then something happened . . . she could be lying in a ditch somewhere—'

'Alan checked the roadsides on his way to work this morning and didn't find anything. So, Mrs Compton, I need to know who her friends are and where I can find them.'

'You're not suggesting she's been deceiving Alan, are you? Meeting someone?'

'No I'm not, and neither is Alan. He's never hinted that, not in the slightest. It's just that if we are to begin finding her, we need to start somewhere. If she's not here, she might have visited a friend yesterday—I need to find her friends and carry my enquiries on from there.'

'Yes, I'm being silly, Mr Rhea, thinking the worst as you do . . . but yes, as I said earlier, she does have friends she visits. I must admit I don't know them too well, but there is that Sylvia Testbury—her husband has that decorating business in Mill Street, the little shop you know. I don't know where she lives but you could ask at the shop. She does the books for the business and they've a retired man comes in to run the shop while Peter Testbury is out at work. Then there's Kay Willison in Harcroft Road and Pat Collins in Newbury Street. . . .'

As she reeled off the names, often without any specific address, I jotted them down in my notebook. I could check with the electoral register at the police station or even the telephone directory—either would help me trace them. I knew that if I visited any of those women, they would probably know the others; they probably got together for morning coffee or tea, or for social outings so it meant I now had several good starting points. But I would begin with Sylvia Testbury.

'I'll start with Mrs Testbury,' I told Jenny's mum. 'Then I want to have words with that bus driver; he could be doing the same run today so I'll have to leave Ashfordly for an hour or so to try and catch him at Gelderslack—I don't want to chase him all over the countryside. If Mrs Testbury can't help, I can trace the others. But I'll keep in touch. If you recall anything, Mrs Compton, can you leave a message for me? You could ring Ashfordly Police Station.'

'I don't have a telephone, Mr Rhea, but I'll ask Phyllis, she's my neighbour, if I can use hers. I'm sure she won't mind, not in the circumstances. And you will let me know what happens, won't you? I shall be so worried about Jenny.'

I assured her I would keep her informed of any developments, then left to visit Sylvia Testbury. I knew the little shop. Tucked away in Mill Street, it occupied a former weaver's cottage whose front and back rooms had been converted into a small shop. It sold items for use in decorating one's home—wallpaper, paste, scrapers, paint and paint brushes, white spirit and anything else remotely associated with visually improving one's own premises. David Testbury had started the shop as a sideline to his business as painter and decorator, paying a retired friend a modest retainer to serve behind the counter and manage the stock because David wanted to continue the painting and decorating side of his business. At home, Sylvia did the books and accounts, and so the small but efficient enterprise was thriving and proving highly popular in Ashfordly. Most of us who liked to paint and decorate our own homes were patrons.

It was while driving to Mill Street that a fleeting thought occurred to me. Alf Ventress had made a passing reference to a painter who had fallen off his ladder to find himself detained in Ashfordly Hospital with broken bones, concussion and maybe a fractured skull. David Testbury was one of the best-known painters and decorators in Ashfordly, but was he likely to let himself fall from a ladder?

I thought he would be sufficiently experienced not to take unnecessary risks but as a policeman, I knew that accidents could happen to anyone at any time. When I arrived at the shop, David's man was behind the counter; his name was Bill Sharpe.

'Hello, Bill. How's things?' I made the usual greeting as I approached the counter. Bill was a small rotund man with a rosy face and a shining bald pate surrounded by tufts of white hair. He wore small, rounded spectacles and a brown apron. He looked completely at home in this tiny shop and reminded me of Mr Pickwick.

'Now then, Mr Rhea. It's a bit quiet at this time of day, but it'll soon pick up. Gives me chance to get my shelves sorted out and stacked, prices on labels, that sort of thing. So what can I do for you? Is it about the boss?'

'Boss?'

'He fell off his ladder yesterday, one hell of a knock; they're worried he might have fractured his skull. A depressed fracture, they think. His missus spent last night in there with him. She hasn't been to see me yet so mebbe she's still up at the hospital, but if she's come home I expect she'll turn up once she's got the kids off to school.'

'That's dreadful! How on earth did he manage that? I would have thought he was too old a hand to fall off a ladder.'

'A pair of dogs were fighting, they banged into his ladder and upskittled it. Luckily, he just missed some iron railings with spikes on.'

'Poor old David, I hope he gets over it. Give him my regards if you see him. But it's Sylvia I've come to see, Bill. I don't know where she lives so I was wondering if you could tell me.'

'Oh aye, Clarendon Street, number twelve. Nice detached house.'

'I'm looking for a friend of hers actually. Jenny Stanwick from Gelderslack, I've a message for her.'

'Oh, right, well, she'll have gone home now, Mr Rhea. Jenny I mean. She was at the house all night, seeing to the kids while Sylvia was in hospital with David—she'll have got 'em off to school by now and gone home I expect. And I expect Sylvia's still at the hospital, wanting to be with David till they know the extent of his injuries. She could be home later but I couldn't give you a time.'

'So Jenny stayed at Clarendon Street last night?'

'Aye, she was having a pub lunch with Sylvia when David had his tumble so she said she'd stay on and look after the children and other things while Sylvia went to hospital with David. When she knew he had to stay in for observations, Sylvia was asked to stay with him all night, he was very poorly, Mr Rhea. They reckon it was touch and go for a while.'

'As bad as that, eh?'

'Oh yes, he was in a bit of a state, that's why they called his wife in.'

'I understand now.'

'Well, when Jenny offered to stay over and see to Sylvia's bairns, she asked me to ring her home at Gelderslack to tell her husband, but I rang and rang, Mr Rhea, all evening and again this morning, but I got no reply. I thought his phone must be out of order. I didn't ring during the night, as I was in bed, and didn't like to ring Jenny to ask her what I should do next in case I woke up the kids. Besides, I reckoned Alan would know where she was.'

'So Alan never got the message?'

'No, not unless Jenny rang him or he rang her, but she'd think I'd've got through, wouldn't she?'

'He told me he was at work then, when he got home, he went out to feed his stock, got washed and changed, then went out at a darts match till late. And he was out early this morning looking for Jenny . . . no wonder none of us could contact him. Which is why I'm here. He's reported Jenny missing.'

'Missing? She's not missing, Mr Rhea, she's been looking after the Testbury kids all night . . . if Alan had answered his phone, he'd have known what was going on. You think he'd have been ringing round anyway, to her friends and so on!'

'He said he didn't want to make a fuss. So does Jenny know you never made contact?'

'No; I haven't seen her this morning, but you'd think she might have rung home herself before now.'

'If she did, she'd get no reply—Alan would be out looking for her! So where will Jenny be now, do you think?'

'I'll ring the house and see if she's there.'

He did, but there was no reply. 'No reply, Mr Rhea. I reckon she'll have gone back to her home now on the bus, leaving Sylvia at the hospital. Then if Sylvia wants more help, Jenny will come back for another session. They are good friends, those two. Like sisters really.'

I looked at my watch.

'I'll drive out to Gelderslack now, I might just catch that bus. I want to see if she's on it!'

And when I arrived in Gelderslack, I was just in time to see Jenny Stanwick getting off the 11 a.m. bus and walking home in her distinctive red coat.

I did not want to alarm or embarrass her by news of our very modest hunt, so I radioed Alf Ventress from my van and told him Jenny Stanwick had returned home safe and sound. It was surprising how many 'Missing From Home' enquiries concluded with the words 'returned home safely.'

'Can you telephone Alan at the abbey?' I asked, not having access to a phone out on those moors. 'Get him to ring home within the next few minutes. I think Jenny had better explain this one to him.'

'Will do,' said Alf in his usual cheerful manner. 'I'm glad she's turned up, Nick, she's a nice woman. So what's the story?'

'I'll tell you when I see you but it's summed up in the old words *lack of communication*,' I said and prepared to finish my transmission. 'But I don't think we need inform our sergeant or anyone else. Thanks for your help in this. Delta Alpha Two Four Over and Out.'

'Control Out,' said Alf.

* * *

This simple tale shows how often we depend on the actions and assistance of others in our daily lives, sometimes without realizing that such help is being given and that it is regularly given quite freely. One problem is that the value of such help is frequently underestimated. On many occasions the helpers don't realize the importance of the assistance they are providing or being asked to provide, which means that if they fail or are careless in some way, the consequences can be more serious than they anticipate. In spite of his earnest efforts, Bill Sharpe failed to contact Alan Stanwick about his wife's unexpected absence and his lapse did not cause great problems, but it might have done. Certainly it created a few hours of concern for both Alan and the local police.

It was a similar story with Jack Carver who owned and ran the Aidensfield Stores. He had bought the business from Oscar Blaketon, Oscar having previously bought it from Joe Steel upon his retirement from the force. Oscar had later sold it and bought the Aidensfield Arms.

The newest owner, Jack, along with his wife Jill, had both previously worked in a department store in Leeds but had always yearned for their own small shop and post office in the countryside. When Aidensfield Stores had come on to the market, therefore, they lost no time in purchasing the business. Within a very few months they had become accepted and liked by the villagers. They sold a bewildering selection of goods ranging from newspapers and magazines to groceries by way of fruit and vegetables, hardware, toiletries, sweets, ice cream, greetings cards, paperback books and other assorted household requirements. They also ran the post office. Their little shop was a true Aladdin's Cave and beyond doubt was one of the main focal points in the community. It was here that local news was disseminated, gossip spread and rumours either denied or confirmed; people would pop into the shop for little more than a chat with friends or to catch up with local news. Just inside the door on the wall was a noticeboard where people could display adverts if they wanted to sell a bicycle or pram, hire a home help or sell their skills in painting, decorating, sewing, gardening, hairdressing or dressmaking.

Living near the shop in a house called Seaton Cottage was a family called Lowson. Stanley and Louise had two teenage children called Danielle and Jonathan who attended secondary school in Ashfordly. Stanley worked in Ashfordly as a travel agent and drove into town each day while his wife worked part-time as a secretary for a local solicitor.

The solicitor, Jeremy Taylor, worked from his spacious home in Maddleskirk where he had an office attached to the house. Louise's job meant she could leave home each morning after all other family members had gone, lock up the house and arrive for work by nine. It was a six or seven minute drive away.

Also, she could leave work at four o'clock in time to be at home when the children came in from school—generally, they returned about quarter past four, with Jeremy arriving around half past five. Sometimes, however, Louise might have to work a few minutes later if her boss was dealing with a very important matter, and sometimes the school bus would return early to Aidensfield. That happened when some of its other passengers stayed late to attend parents' evenings, sports events or theatrical practice. Due to bypassing just one of the small villages on the route back to Aidensfield from Ashfordly, the bus could shorten its journey by fifteen or twenty minutes, hence the occasional early return to Aidensfield for the village children, including the Lowsons.

These minor blips in the daily routine of the Lowson family could have caused problems had it not been for the consideration provided by the successive owners of Aidensfield Stores. The Lowsons' problem was they had only one key to their cottage. Of considerable age, Seaton Cottage had two massive doors, one at the back and the other at the front; both were secured by gigantic mortise locks, each served by the same key. And they had only one key.

The key was about seven inches long (13cm) and made from solid iron; it had an oval grip at one end while the portion which operated the mechanism of the locks was an inch and a half square (4cm) with a somewhat intricate design. It was the sort of key one might expect to find in a cathedral door or the gateway to a castle and for some reason, none of the previous owners of Seaton Cottage had obtained a duplicate.

And neither had the Lowsons, probably because its huge size meant it was unlikely to be mislaid or lost. Furthermore, it would require a skilled blacksmith or metalworker to recreate such a monster, or to copy it accurately from the original. A slight error could mean any substitute key might not function. Thus for more years than anyone could recall, Seaton Cottage never had more than one key.

Locking and unlocking the house in association with the comings and goings of the family members at different times therefore presented a continuing but minor difficulty. The Lowsons did not like to leave such a large key under a stone near the front door and there was nowhere else to safely conceal it. The answer was to leave it at the shop which was open every day from 6.30 a.m. until 8 p.m. The procedure was that the last person to leave the house therefore followed the long-standing practice of leaving Seaton Cottage key at Aidensfield Stores. It was safe there and it meant that family members returning to the happy home could collect it whenever they wished.

Successive shopkeepers had been happy to co-operate with the Lowsons and their predecessors, so when any of them deposited the key in the shop, it would be placed safely under the counter until collected. If the key wasn't in the shop, it meant one of the family had it in their possession. That was the simple logic of the operation.

But we should always bear in mind that it was Robbie Burns (1759-1796) who wrote 'The best laid schemes o' mice an' men gang aft a-gley,' which, when translated into English, means 'the best laid plans of mice and men often go astray.'

Because the key-leaving custom of Seaton Cottage had never been known to go wrong, everyone assumed it could and would continue indefinitely without any problems. And so it was one Wednesday morning that Stanley had left for work around 8.15 a.m. and the children had gone to catch their school bus at 8.30 a.m. That left Louise to lock up before going to work. She busied herself tidying up for a few minutes and then the telephone rang; it was merely a friend checking on some previous arrangement but it occupied her for a few precious minutes. When she left the house for work, therefore, she was in a hurry. She rushed into the shop where Jill Carver was serving a customer; the customer was paying for her purchases and her large canvas carrier bag was on the floor at her feet and very close to the counter. It was full of groceries, fruit and vegetables, all in individual brown paper bags.

Other customers were milling around and the place was at its usual busy best, so Louise plonked the key on a pile of newspapers which stood on the counter, waved at Jill and hurried off. Jill acknowledged her with a smile. They had undertaken that small action time and time again.

Even before the customer had received her change, a man rushed into the shop, grabbed the topmost newspaper from the pile, plonked the correct money on the place where the paper had been, and hurried away. Unknown to him and to anyone else the key slid off as he lifted the paper and it dropped into the carrier bag below, not making a sound because it landed among the assorted paper bags, then slid gently to the bottom.

Having paid for her purchases, the lady customer left the shop with her full bag, not realizing the key was now lying at the bottom. It was likely that when she reached home, she would lift out her purchases in their bags, and never notice the key. The incident went unnoticed until the children returned from school late that afternoon. They arrived from the bus and, as always, went into the shop both to collect the key and buy some sweets with their pocket money.

'Sorry, the key's not here,' said Jack Carver. 'Your mum must have got home first.'

The children went home, only a few yards from the shop, but Seaton Cottage was locked and there was no sign of Louise.

Thinking their mum might have popped in to see a friend, the children sat on the doorstep to enjoy their sweets; fortunately it was a mild and dry afternoon. Louise arrived from work about twenty minutes later.

'Aren't you going in?' she asked.

'No, it's locked. Haven't you got the key?' Danielle acted as spokesperson.

'No, I thought you would have collected it.'

'It's not there; we went for it but it's not there.'

'It must be! I left it this morning. You wait there, I'll go and check.'

When Louise insisted she had left the key on top of a pile of newspapers before going to work this morning, reminding Jack that Jill was behind the counter at the time, it resulted in a search of all the shelves, drawers, cupboards and floor, but of the key there was no trace. It was too big to slip down a gap in the floorboards or get wedged between a couple of bean tins or jam jars on a shelf. As the puzzle developed into something more serious—such as a family being locked out of their home—Jill came down from the flat above where she was preparing the evening meal, but said she hadn't seen the key. She did recall Louise being in the shop that morning and waving at her, but had no recollection of seeing the key or placing it in a safe place. This resulted in Louise frantically searching her handbag, pockets and briefcase without result.

'Has Stanley been home during the day?' asked Jack. 'He might have picked it up.'

'I've no idea, I suppose he could have come for something and then forgotten to return the key . . .'

'Ring him,' offered Jack. 'Use our phone.'

But Stanley had not come home during the day and could not offer any explanation about the missing key. He felt sure Louise must have been mistaken—a key that size could not vanish without trace, so had she checked that the house really was locked? Or had it been unlocked all day? Had she merely *thought* she'd secured the house this morning? Louise promised she would make another check.

She returned to the waiting children and tried to open the front door, but it was firmly locked, as were all the windows, upstairs and down. Then she made Jonathan climb over the high gate which prevented unauthorized access to the rear of the house and garden, asking him to test the back door but also to see if any of the rear windows were open, especially those upstairs. He returned to say everything was secure. They were locked out.

Louise was beginning to panic by this stage. There seemed no answer to their predicament, other than to break in through one of the ground-floor windows but even if they did so, both doors would remain firmly locked. Breaking in would not really solve the problem, and she did not like to take that kind of drastic action without Stanley's approval—better still, perhaps he would come home and sort out the problem? She decided to ring him, not from the shop this time, but from the village kiosk.

It was at this point, before she made that call, that I arrived on the scene. I was on a routine patrol of the village when I saw the family standing outside the front door looking distressed and most uneasy, so I stopped to see if I could help.

'Something wrong?' I asked.

'We're locked out,' said Danielle, with all the simplicity that only a child can produce. 'Mum's lost the key.'

'I haven't lost the key,' she snapped. 'I left it at the shop, as I always do, but they say it isn't there. They've searched high and low . . . and Stanley hasn't got it either. I definitely left it at the shop, Mr Rhea, before I went to work this morning. That's what I always do.'

'Oh dear.' My heart sank. My first concern was that someone might have stolen it—but would a thief know which door it would fit? A local person might, but I did not think we had such thieves in Aidensfield. Nonetheless, getting hold of the key to premises was the simplest method of breaking in and if a householder did suspect the door key had been stolen, it was vital they changed the locks without delay. 'So what happened? Do you know?'

It was then that Louise told me the story, highlighting the fact it was their only key and emphasizing its huge size. I felt her account had a strong ring of truth. Certainly, neither Jack nor Jill would stoop to stealing a neighbour's key, and I was sure that neither would anyone living in Aidensfield. So had there been a thief about? A travelling rogue?

If there had, perhaps something else had disappeared from the shop without being noticed? Shoplifters operated very quickly, often under cover of other distractions and so I said I would carry out enquiries.

'Oh, but you mustn't let them think I suspect them in the shop, Mr Rhea . . . that would be dreadful . . . I mean, it's an act of kindness when they take in our key. I don't want them to think I am complaining or accusing them of anything. I was just going to ring Stanley to ask him to come home early; he'll know what to do. I was thinking of breaking in but that doesn't get the doors open!'

'Leave it with me for just a few minutes, don't ring Stanley just yet,' I suggested. 'If you left it at the shop, the chances are it will still be there, particularly if there's not been a thief about. I'll ask—and I will be diplomatic, I assure you.'

She agreed, albeit with evident reluctance, so I went along to the shop, asking the family to continue their vigil outside the front door for a few more minutes. Fortunately, there were no customers in when I entered, so, as a form of modest subterfuge, I bought some sweets, ostensibly for my own children.

'I've just seen the Lowsons outside their house,' I commented. 'I think they're locked out.'

Jill answered. 'They are. They always leave their key here when everyone's out. It's huge, not the sort you would overlook, but Louise said she put it on a pile of newspapers this morning, then rushed off to work. We had a good look around, there's no sign of it. We always put it under the counter for safekeeping.'

'Have you had thieves in?' I asked. 'Shoplifters?'

'No, not today. Everyone's been local, we know them all. There've been no strangers in.'

'So what time did Louise leave it?'

'Just before nine this morning, that's her usual time. If there are customers at the counter, she just plonks it on top of the pile of newspapers at the end and we see to it. That's been the custom since before we came here.'

'And were there customers?'

'Yes, I was busy with Mrs Atkinson, she always comes in early and buys her groceries, and yes, I remember, a man rushed in while I was serving her, he grabbed a paper from the pile and left the money on top of the others . . . he must have disturbed the key! I never thought of that till now.'

'Disturbed the key? How, do you think?'

'Well, if he lifted the paper, the key would slide off and fall either on the counter or on the floor. It's not behind the counter and not on the counter; I've looked, we've *all* looked . . . if it did fall, though, we would have heard it, it's a massive iron key.'

'Did you check this side of the counter?'

'No, we didn't . . . but if that key had fallen down there, somebody would have heard it, or it might have landed on their foot! Nobody could miss it, that's for sure.'

'What about Mrs Atkinson? Where was she while all this was going on?'

'She was paying for her things . . . ah, now then, Mr Rhea. Her carrier bag was on the floor, beside her feet, directly below those newspapers . . . that's where she always puts it while I'm serving her. I wonder if it fell in there? It's a big canvas bag with a wide open top.'

'Would she know if it did slide into her bag?'

'Maybe not. All her fruit and veg and so on were in brown paper bags, so if it fell into her carrier she might never know, unless she found it when she unpacked.'

'It's a possibility, Jill. Thanks. I'll tell the Lowsons—then go and have words with Mrs Atkinson. I hope she doesn't think I'm accusing her of being a shoplifter and potential housebreaker!'

And so the riddle was solved. When I went to see Mrs Atkinson, she had not found the key, but when she fished around in the bottom of her bag, among her scarves, head squares and gloves, she found the key. It was nestling among her belongings and might have remained there for months, had we not asked her to search for it.

As a result of that incident, the Lowsons approached a locksmith in Ashfordly to fit a pair of more modern locks to their doors, along with plenty of spare keys. They made a special glass-fronted display case for their old key and it now hangs in their front hall with both old locks beside it. But they continued to leave one of the spare keys in the shop, just in case any of the family was locked out.

CHAPTER THREE

If there had been a prize for the worst view in and around the North York Moors, it would surely have been awarded to Claude Jeremiah Greengrass for the state of his paddock at Hagg Bottom. Barely a blade of grass could be seen in that part of the Greengrass ranch—it was piled high and almost completely smothered with all manner of junk, ancient, not-so-ancient, modern and of uncertain vintage. This once-green part of his ramshackle homestead had been transformed into the combination of a rubbish dump, council tip, scrap-yard and depository for unwanted farm implements, household goods and motor vehicle spare parts. The place was full of things which Claude felt might become useful one day, such as old toilets, baths, car seats, prams, mangles, a pile of old horseshoes, ploughs, wardrobes, armchairs, settees, carpets, kitchen cabinets, complete but immobile cars and motor-bikes, lorry engines, tyres, several old caravans, a henhouse or two, corrugated iron sheets, spare parts for almost everything and a host of other useless, rusting and broken objects which he had assembled or which had probably been dumped there by other people.

Nothing ever seemed to leave this dumping ground. Instead, more and more stuff arrived on a fairly regular basis, most of it acquired by Claude during his forays into the depths of the countryside. I think some of it was payment for services rendered—if Claude performed a task for a farmer or householder, he was often in the practice of accepting goods in lieu of a cash payment.

This had two advantages. It was a tax-free method of doing business and he also hoped to dispose of the acquired object for a handsome profit—through a cash sale, of course! That was the theory—but it seldom worked like that. It usually meant Claude was stuck with an object that no one else would buy, not even for its spare parts. Once a thing arrived on his pile, it generally remained there.

His infamous collection of rubbish therefore grew bigger and bigger. It followed that if any unusual thefts occurred in the locality, the first place to be examined by the police was the Greengrass paddock at Hagg Bottom. Even if Greengrass had not stolen the item in question (he was not a common thief), there was always the likelihood he might have bought it from the thief, either innocently, or even in the hope it might not be stolen property. Not surprisingly, there were frequent occasions when a search of his mountain of junk was considered necessary. Sometimes it was done by me or one of the other Ashfordly officers, and sometimes it involved detectives from Divisional Headquarters. These searches were fairly routine but such was the state of the dump that it was difficult to find anything specific—in many ways, the Greengrass ranch was the perfect hiding place for stolen property. The truth was, however, that even if stolen goods were thought to have been concealed there, the difficult task was actually finding them. Quite simply, there was far too much clutter and too many places to conceal things. I am sure Claude had no idea what was really kept on his premises—his pile of junk had been growing there for years and years.

Although Claude would never hide stolen goods there, others might. It was the practice among thieves to conceal their ill-gotten goods as soon as possible after the crime had been committed. This meant that if the police did catch them quickly and make a search of their home or vehicle, no incriminating evidence would be found. It made sense to hide things as soon as possible. Later, when the investigation and police search had cooled down, the thieves would return to their hiding place to recover the cache of goods and sell them.

Unfortunately, I am sure many thieves considered Claude's cluttered paddock a very useful hiding place. So vast was its area and so deep its collection of assorted junk that most things could be safely concealed without even Claude knowing or suspecting their presence. I am sure a stolen lorry could be driven into Claude's paddock and covered with other junk so that no one would realize it was there. Very large and very small things could be easily concealed and to complete a thorough search literally involved moving a mountain. One snag was that there was nowhere else to put the stuff, except back on the mountain where it probably concealed something else. Smaller items such as portable radio sets, cameras, vases, candlesticks, various antiques and artworks could be securely hidden among Claude's collection—without anyone knowing. And that, of course, could put Claude firmly under suspicion in the possible event of any stolen goods being discovered on his plot.

For all his deviousness, however, I knew Claude was not a thief—certainly he had an eye for a bargain and he would cheerfully remove junk to his pile of rubbish in the hope of making a few shillings, but he did not steal and he would never break into anyone's home or premises. He might deal in property others had obtained by less-than-honest methods, but among his colleagues, that was regarded as a weakness in the owner of the goods. Claude would not knowingly handle stolen goods either. I knew that, but incoming police officers did not; not surprisingly, there were times I found myself protecting Claude against unfair allegations on those rare occasions when stolen goods were found dumped among his rubbish.

I was also aware of the possibility that unscrupulous visitors—thieves in other words—would remove items from Claude's paddock, generally under cover of darkness and without his knowledge or consent. Sometimes he was happy for this to happen—if he could not get rid of something large and unwanted, then he was happy for a thief to spirit it away, but on some occasions he would arrive home with a ghastly object on his truck, knowing he had a customer who wanted exactly such a thing. That is how he made some of his money and people would frequently ask him to look out for specific but unusual objects. Consequently if he did find something special or unique, and the thing was then stolen before it reached Claude's customer, he had lost that part of his permanently unreliable income.

What it all added up to, of course, was that upon my quiet rural patch, there was a small paddock seething with secret criminality—thieves and rogues haunting the place to either dump their ill-gotten goods, to hide them or even to steal from Claude. However, if Claude did have something stolen from his pile, it was only very rarely that he made a formal report to the police. On most occasions, he would sort out the problem by himself, generally knowing who had taken the object, where to find it and how to deal with the culprit. One official problem with thefts from Claude was that the missing items could rarely be positively identified or even described with any degree of accuracy, and that made detection by the police almost impossible.

Claude knew that, and so, apart from occasional official searches to satisfy police records and to keep Claude on his toes, we enjoyed a kind of ongoing truce so far as nefarious activities by others affected his ever-present and ever-expanding pile of junk.

It was with some surprise, therefore, that I answered the doorbell of my police house shortly after nine one morning to find an agitated Claude Jeremiah Greengrass on the doorstep. As it happened, I was on duty but was working in my office to catch up with some paperwork which had to be taken to Ashfordly Police Station for checking by the sergeant before being forwarded to Eltering Sub-Division.

'Ah, Claude, good morning.'

'Not got you out of bed, have I?' he asked, with that cheeky grin of his.

'No, not even though I was on duty until one o'clock this morning,' I responded to his banter. 'Checking that my parishioners—including you—were secure in their beds and safe from thieves, murderers, rapists, highwaymen and others. So what brings you here at this time of day?'

'A thief, that's what. Somebody's been nicking from my stock of valuable saleable commodities.'

'Really?'

'Aye, really. And I mean really. So if you were out and about last night, watching out for thieves, why didn't you catch him?'

'Perhaps he was watching me and nicked your stuff when I came home. Or perhaps he did it another time.'

'You blokes always have an answer—'

'Only because there is an answer!'

'Well, whatever your excuse for letting me be the victim of crime, I want to report it.'

'Fair enough. You'd better come in.'

I led him into my office and settled him on a chair next to my desk, then got out my notepad and statement forms.

'So, Claude, this is a rare occasion, you visiting me. It's usually the other way round. Now, do you fancy a cup of tea? I don't normally offer that to visitors, but I think this is a very special occasion.'

'Well, if it's that special, then yes. With milk and two sugars. And I wouldn't say no to a jam tart or a biscuit or two.'

While Mary boiled the kettle and found some biscuits, I settled down with my papers and began to interview him.

'So, Claude, what's been stolen?'

'My door-knockers.'

'Door-knockers? Both of them, you mean?'

'Both? No, I don't mean those on the house. I mean those I've been collecting. From folks having doorbells fitted. All the rage are doorbells, folks getting themselves modernized. You can hear them better inside the house and they don't knock on the door by themselves when gales are blowing on these moors. You can sleep without thinking somebody's trying to wake you up in the middle of the night. So folks have been getting rid of their door-knockers; it's been going on for years now. I've been collecting them, I've got loads . . . well, I had loads, until somebody came and nicked them.'

'So if everybody else has been getting rid of their knockers, why were you collecting them?'

'To melt 'em down, constable, for scrap metal. There's allus a demand for good quality scrap, and most of 'em are iron or brass . . . or I might keep the best of 'em in case they become antiques one day. I get 'em for nowt, folks just want rid of them so whatever happens to 'em, I make a profit. There's good money in door-knockers, Constable Rhea.'

'Unless somebody nicks them?' I said.

'Aye, which brings us back to why I'm here. Like I said, somebody has nicked 'em; taken the lot.'

'So how many are we talking about?'

'A couple of tons or thereabouts. A good lorryload at least.'

'Two tons?'

'Aye, summat like that. There's a few years' collecting represented in that lot. There's no point in taking scrap metal to be melted down by the pocketful or barrowload; to make it worthwhile you need lorryloads, and plenty of loads, all big 'uns. I've been building up my collection over the years, enough to make a lorry load, two and a half or three tons, summat like that.'

'So how many knockers are we talking about?'

'Dunno to be exact. How much does one weigh? A couple of pounds? That's seven to a stone, fifty-six to a hundredweight which means one thousand, one hundred and twenty to a ton. Roughly. I reckon I had two tons waiting so that's two thousand two hundred and forty knockers, give and take a few here and there because of their different weights.'

'A lot of knockers,' was all I could think of saying.

'A lot of money an' all,' he grunted.

'You'll be insured?' I put to him.

'Insured? You must be joking. What insurance company would cover me when I leave stuff outside to God and providence. No, Constable, there's no insurance. I'm not reporting this to get a pay-out from the insurance man, I'm reporting it because it's a sneaky thing to do, nicking my stock of knockers. It's dishonest! It makes me sick! There was I, waiting for the day I could take a lorryload to be melted down and get myself a nice little earner, and when I went to check this morning, they'd all gone. The lot. So I want you to find them.'

'So can you describe them? What do they look like?'

'Look like? What do you mean? They're door-knockers; they look like door-knockers. A thing to get hold of and a back-plate to hammer it against, and a hinge to hold 'em together. Holes for screws. Some might have door paint on, or splashes if the painter wasn't up to his job. Most are iron, and some are brass. I thought most folks would know what a door-knocker looks like.'

'Fair enough, so can you identify them?' was my next question.

'Identify them? Each one, you mean?'

'Well, if we catch somebody with a lorryload of knockers, how can we prove they're yours? One door-knocker is very much like another.'

'Well, who else round here would have two tons or more of knockers?'

'Some other scrap dealer who has an eye for the main chance . . . who's seen the potential in selling scrap door-knockers to be melted down—'

'Who is likely to have pinched all mine, you mean!'

'We'd have to prove they were yours. Anyway, next question Claude. When did they disappear?'

'How do I know? If I'd seen 'em going, I'd have done summat to stop it!'

At this point, Mary came in with the tea and biscuits, enough for the pair of us, and so we filled our cups and I resumed my questions.

'I need to know when they were stolen. If you can't give a precise date, I need to know when you last saw them, and when you realized they'd gone. Were they stolen during last night, for example?'

'It was this morning when I noticed they'd gone. But don't ask me when I last saw them, I've no idea. I've been adding to my collection for years, like I said . . . one here, one there . . .'

'Was it Christmas when you saw them?'

'Nay, since then. Easter mebbe.'

'So, if I say they were stolen between Good Friday and today, that should cover it? That's nearly six months. It doesn't help us catch the thieves, Claude, they could have had the stuff melted down months ago. They might have been taken any time since Easter. You should have reported this to us earlier. It doesn't give us much chance to find the thieves or the stolen goods.'

'Aye, mebbe, but that is your job, isn't it? Recovering stolen property. Look, while you're asking all these questions and filling those forms in, they could be out there on the road, heading for a furnace somewhere . . . you should be out there, looking for 'em.'

'We'll check all the furnaces and scrap dealers in this region, Claude, but you know as well as me that once that metal has been melted down, we've no chance of finding the villains.'

'Aye, well, I thought you might alert all your foot patrols and motor patrols and detectives and special constables and traffic wardens and control rooms and police headquarters and Scotland Yard and all the rest of your lot, to catch 'em red-handed, with the loot.' He blinked furiously.

'I will notify all those people and they will keep their eyes open, but I need some background first, which is why I am asking all these questions and filling in these forms. A few minutes spent getting the facts is very important; it's better than chasing around the countryside like a headless chicken. So what's the value of the stolen goods?'

'Whatever I can get for 'em.'

'I need a stated value, Claude.'

'How do I know what they're worth? I only know that when I get paid for selling 'em, and that's not going to happen by the look of things.'

'All right, what's a new knocker cost?'

'Search me, I've never bought one.'

'A pound? Fifteen shillings? Thirty bob?'

'I'd say about thirty bob, Constable. Maybe more depending on quality and what it's made of. Some less, some more. Most of mine are antiques; I reckon they'll be worth more than new 'uns.'

'That's good enough for me; you're the expert,' I said. 'So two thousand two hundred and forty knockers at one pound ten shillings each comes to a grand total of—'

'Three thousand three hundred and sixty quid,' he said in a flash.

'Crumbs,' I breathed. 'That's more than three years' wages for me!'

'They don't pay you in door-knockers though, do they?' he chuckled. 'That's my pay, not for just one year but for dozens . . . I've been collecting those knockers for years, Constable and thought it was time I realized some of my assets. And they've all gone up in smoke. Every single one. A lifetime's work vanished in a flash . . .'

'All right, Claude, I get the message. Right, I'll telephone details through to Ashfordly Police Station so we can circulate the crime as quickly as we can, and then I'll have to come and visit the scene.'

'Visit the scene? There's no point in doing that, the stuff's gone!'

'We have to visit the scene of every crime, Claude, and this is a crime. For one thing, we must inspect it for any likely evidence that's been left behind . . . there are all sorts of other reasons for visiting scenes of crime.'

'Aye, well, you know your job. So what do I do now?'

'Ask around. Talk to your pals and contacts, tell them what's happened. See if anyone's been offering door-knockers on the cheap, see if any lorries were seen around your yard during the night . . . there's a lot you can be doing.'

'Aye, right. I mean, I didn't want to take jobs off you fellers, 'cos I thought you and your mates would be doing all that sort of thing. Asking around, checking thieves and scrappies, searching wagons and such.'

'We will, but the more people ask around and talk about it, the better chance we have to detecting your crime and recovering your property. Now, about my visit to the scene. When would be convenient?'

'Suit yourself, Constable. You know where it is. Just get yourself there and have a snoop around—you've done it umpteen times before so you know what's what, and I can tell you there's no nicked property there. It's all legitimate, every scrap of it.'

'You should be there, Claude, I might have some questions to ask. And I want to know which part of your premises they were stolen from.'

'You know where they were stolen from. I've just spent ages telling you.'

'I mean the precise place. That site of yours is quite large.'

'Well, I can't help today. I'm a busy chap as you know and from here, I'm going straight off to Redcar because there's a sale of fairground roundabouts and dodgems that might be interesting, and then on the way home I'm popping into that saleroom at Guisborough where I hear they've got some old fireplaces that'll be auctioned off next week . . . so just help yourself, Constable.'

'I'll go now, but I might have to come back if I've any queries.'

'Well, that's up to you. You can walk round my site in a few minutes, it's not all that large, and you'll see whatever you want—minus two tons of second-hand door-knockers.'

'Fair enough, I know the place fairly well. You do whatever you must, and I'll set the official wheels in motion.'

'Right, but you will keep me informed, won't you? If you come up with any news? There's a lot of money at stake here. It could mean my company's profit for the year has gone up in smoke.'

'Of course, Claude, and I trust you'll do likewise. Keep me informed if anything new comes up, I mean. If you hear anything, don't keep it to yourself, you'll not be grassing on your mates, you'll be helping to solve a serious crime.'

'Mebbe I should have joined the force; I think I can solve crimes faster than you lot . . .'

'Then this is a good chance to put yourself to the test, Claude, with all those contacts of yours.'

At that stage, we parted, Claude going about his daily business while I finalized my report, rang Alf Ventress at Ashfordly Police Station to set in motion the circulation of a description of Claude's missing items, and then settled down to finish my other paperwork. As some of the files were important, I would have to deliver them to Ashfordly Police Station before heading off to the Greengrass ranch, and I could also present my initial crime report.

About an hour later, having visited Ashfordly to deposit my reports, record the crime, enter it in the necessary police files and circulate details throughout the region, I drove out to Hagg Bottom. At this stage, of course, I had no suspects and not even the vaguest of descriptions of a possible culprit or suspect vehicle. Hopefully I would discover something during my forthcoming enquiries. I told Alf Ventress where I was heading next; he would inform Sergeant Craddock who was currently visiting Eltering Sub-Divisional Headquarters, a regular conference of supervisory officers.

'Do you need Scenes of Crime to come out and examine the scene?' asked Alf. 'Photographs, fingerprints, that sort of thing.'

'I don't think so, Alf. The place is a veritable tip! The stuff could have been taken six months ago or more, so that would be waste of their time. Even so, I might change my mind after visiting the scene—I'm on my way there now.'

And so I motored out to Hagg Bottom, not relishing the task of searching for clues among Claude's junk. The moment I crested the hill I could see his spread below. The old house, looking as ancient as the moorland itself, lay snug in a hollow, free from the worst of the winds and on the edge of a patch of grass. Behind was the heather, thick and almost impenetrable except for creatures like the blackfaced sheep and grouse.

I drove slowly down the unmade track, my police van bumping along and scraping its exhaust on protruding rocks until I reached the area in front of the house. Here vehicles turned around or parked and so I reversed in, set the handbrake and switched off the engine. When I climbed out, I could smell the distinctive scent of the heather despite the combination of puzzling whiffs emanating from Claude's tip, and was pleased the ever-present breeze was blowing. It made things nice and fresh.

As I walked towards the massive pile of junk, I realized its appearance had altered since my last visit but, for a few minutes, couldn't see how or where those changes were. Perhaps some stuff had been taken away and more taken its place—that was the most logical explanation. However, as I began to stride around its boundaries I realized there were no broad aisles between the piles, just a few narrow gaps—the only way to gain access to the centre was to clamber over the clutter, but I decided against that. It was too dangerous—I could find myself struggling to negotiate some large object that might move or collapse beneath me and, with Claude absent, I could find myself trapped or injured with no help available. All I could do was complete a tour of the site at ground level, hoping I might find some clue as to the disappearance of Claude's door-knockers.

As I reached the far side, I found my first clue. It was an almost circular patch of bare earth with a diameter of almost six feet containing a few straggly bits of whitened grass or weeds and, because it was surrounded by good green grass devoid of junk, highly distinctive. This must be the place from which the door-knockers had been stolen. It made sense to have stocked them here. This site could be approached by a vehicle of some kind but when I searched for signs of tyre marks, I found none that could be identified. The place was full of wheel marks, most of which would be Claude's or those of his genuine visitors. But, as I was examining the scene, head down in my efforts to identity anything unusual or noteworthy, I found a door-knocker. As I glanced at it, I realized it was lying on the ground at the edge of the site—and it was in one of those narrow gaps. I managed to reach it and pick it up and then saw another, further into the heap of junk, but also lying on the ground in a small space. Had the thief dropped these in his rush to escape with his cache? But those spaces were far too narrow to admit a motor vehicle or even a wheelbarrow—even someone on foot would have difficulty finding a way through.

The access was little more than a few inches wide but I could move along it and so I did, picking my way carefully over the odd lump of ironware which lay in my path. And I found other door-knockers, all made of iron and all clearly very old and disused. After trekking for about ten yards, I came to an old relic of a caravan whose undercarriage had collapsed and whose door was now standing wide open.

And when I looked inside, it was full of door-knockers, with many having slid out to form a miniature pile on the ground. There was little wonder the caravan had collapsed, the weight must have been enormous. The proverbial last knocker that broke the caravan's back. I wondered if Claude's entire two tons were kept in here. Clearly, someone had walked past the caravan and accidentally kicked one or two of the escaped door-knockers, sending them ahead on the ground but my question now was whether these were Claude's entire stock or whether others had been stolen.

And he wasn't here to ask!

In my official notebook I recorded what I had found and returned to my normal patrolling duties, unable to proceed with the enquiry as I was not in a position to clarify the matter due to Claude's absence. Until I could, however, I would not halt the circulation of the stolen door-knockers. After all, Claude might have had other stocks of them.

During the rest of that day's patrolling around my Aidensfield patch I asked questions around all the villages at which I called, but failed to find anyone who could throw any light on the mystery. I booked off duty at 5 p.m., a rare event because it meant an evening at home, but as I was settling down to my tea with the family, there was a loud knocking at my front door—not the office door. When I answered it, Claude was standing there, blinking at me through his whiskers and hair.

'I'm on my way home,' he said. 'I just wondered if you'd found them knockers of mine.'

'Yes, I think I have,' and it was obvious that my words surprised him. I invited him into the office and he followed me with evident signs of eagerness.

'You mean that? You're not having me on?'

'Would I do that, Claude? To be honest, I just *think* I have found them—as I said earlier, we can't really distinguish one knocker from another but I'd say I could have found up to two tons of them, all safe and sound.'

'You'll have got the thief inside then? Where he deserves to be?'

'No, Claude.'

'But you have found my stuff?'

'As I said, I think I have. I'm not sure.'

'You're playing games with me, Constable Rhea. What are you trying to cover up?'

'Where did you store your knockers?'

'Well, all over the spot. I haven't got a special place . . . oh . . . mebbe I have . . . I forgot . . .' and I knew by the expression on his face that he now recalled the hiding place.

'Go on, Claude.'

'They're there, aren't they? You've found 'em on my land . . .'

'In an old caravan, Claude. It's undercarriage has collapsed under the weight, and knockers are spilling out . . . now, have you another store of them?'

'No,' he said meekly. 'That's the lot. Look, I'm sorry about this . . . I mean, sending you off on a wild goose chase.'

'Claude, you asked me to find your door-knockers. I've done that. End of story.'

'Aye, well, I don't know what to say, Constable.'

'Then say nowt, Claude. But there is one other thing.'

'Yes?'

'I found a circular patch on that area of grass behind your tip, as if something's been removed, something that's been standing there for a long time. At first, I thought it might be where your pile of door-knockers had been sited, but clearly it wasn't. So what's gone from there, Claude?'

As I described the location in more detail, I could see his mind was working hard and then he said, 'You say there's nowt there?'

'Nothing, Claude, except a patch of bare ground.'

'Then somebody's pinched 'em!'

'Pinched what, Claude?'

'My pile of horseshoes! I had a pile of horseshoes there, gathered over the years ready for what I can take 'em to be melted down . . . at least two tons, Constable. Now who would nick two tons of horseshoes?'

'That's a good question. So do you want to make an official report?'

'You bet I do. You might come across 'em in your travels.'

'So long as they're not hidden somewhere among all that junk of yours . . .'

'Aye, well, mebbe I'd better go and have a look, hadn't I? I might have put 'em somewhere safe and forgotten where . . .'

'Squirrels do that, Claude.'

'Do what?'

'Hide nuts and acorns and forget where they've put them. Anyway, you go and have a look round and if you can't find them, come back and make an official report, then we'll make another search. Meanwhile, I will cancel your report of theft of the door-knockers and record it as "no crime".'

'Aye, right,' he said, and turned to shuffle out of my office. 'Oh, and thanks, I didn't mean to be a nuisance.'

'No problem, Claude,' and, as he returned to his old lorry, I went into the house to continue my tea. He never returned to report the theft of his horseshoes but whenever I went to his house, I could not see them. In time, the bare patch of ground became covered with new grass but I must admit I wondered where he might have hidden two tons of used horseshoes. I think he had another old caravan on his site, but I never went to make a search. I never knew what I might find.

The curious disappearance of Claude's pile of horseshoes, which was never recorded as a crime, reminded me of other curious thefts. For some obscure reason, thieves are prone to stealing women's underwear from washing lines (what on earth do they do with the stolen items?) but other thefts within the Aidensfield area during the 1960s were equally bizarre. One included an entire lawn, newly laid by a proud houseowner, then 500 water lilies vanished from a small lake at a stately home. Someone stole a 300 foot high chimney; another stole an iron footbridge; while yet more managed to get away with several hundred yards of railway track.

Over the period of just a few months, there was a spate of thefts of large vehicles such as road rollers, bulldozers, trench diggers, cement mixers and lorries. We never understood why this should suddenly arise, but perhaps it could be associated with the theft of three prefabricated houses, a few greenhouses, an entire front porch, a collector's stock of manhole covers, the entire collection of fireplaces from an empty country house, all the carpets from another empty house and several instances of new bathroom suites removed from building sites.

Perhaps the most curious were two instances where false teeth were stolen. One set vanished from the bedside glass belonging to a wearer—his home was broken into during the night and next morning, he found his teeth had been taken. It was thought they appealed to the thief because of the gold they contained.

This made some sense—unlike a woman who fell asleep open-mouthed in her car when parked on a layby; she awoke to find her false teeth had been stolen.

One difficulty in prosecuting thieves was that property found in their possession had to be positively identified as that which had been stolen. This could be difficult—for example, one gents' blue Raleigh bicycle with a 21" frame is just like many others unless an owner personalizes it in some way; a £5 note is just like any other unless the owner knows its serial number, while clothing removed from a shop might be exactly the same as any other clothing for sale on the premises. Why, therefore, would people steal village name signs from their sites and, more curiously, why steal that famous railway station name-plate, the longest in Britain, which reads Llanfairpwllgwyngyllgogerychwyrndrobwllllantysiliogogogoch? That could be identified very easily, I would think. Of course, railway engines have also been subjected to theft as have buses, coaches, cars, bicycles, motorbikes, caravans, aircraft and ships, not to mention famous statues, a set of gallows and several hearses, some with a corpse on board.

With strange thefts of this kind coming to our attention either through our own internal police circulars or perhaps via the daily newspapers, it might be argued that nothing surprises the police. Quite simply, determined thieves will nick anything. On most occasions, the theft would be a means of raising some illicit cash—it was often said that without dealers in stolen property, there would be no thieves.

This is not entirely true because some people steal so that they can make personal use of the stolen goods, or alternatively acquire belongings that no one else possesses—like the unique Welsh station name-plate mentioned earlier.

Perhaps the most puzzling theft to come my way as the constable of Aidensfield was reported by Mr Geoffrey Wardle, a local landowner. He owned large tracts of land along the southern edge of the North York Moors, a high percentage of it being upland with a thick covering of heather and bracken. It was not really the sort of land one would normally cultivate, the predominant reason for owning such acres being that they were ideal for either sheep rearing or grouse shooting. However, thanks to modern developments in the shape of giant forest ploughs towed by powerful caterpillar tractors, this kind of rough landscape could be cultivated, albeit for a very limited range of crops. In some cases, it meant ploughing deep enough to remove an underlying layer of peat, up to a few feet thick, which prevented water from penetrating to the earth below. This layer produced a very dry surface in summer but marshland in winter and so in some cases special drainage ploughs were utilized. In short, it meant that previously inhospitable ground could, with considerable effort, produce crops of trees that would survive the harsh environment of the moors. Inevitably, these were conifers, mainly spruce, and so, over the years, parts of the North York Moors became afforested, usually thanks to the efforts of the Forestry Commission, but also due to the determination of a few private landowners.

Geoffrey Wardle was a familiar figure in and around the Ashfordly-Aidensfield area. With an aristocratic background, he was a man of considerable wealth and foresight, a regular attender of agricultural shows, seminars, machinery demonstrations, shooting parties and hunt meets. In his early fifties and of stocky build with a florid, happy face, he had a mop of sandy hair that always looked windswept, and inevitably wore dark-brown plus fours with thick socks and brogue shoes. His permanent companion, apart from his golden Labrador called Ben, was a hazel stick with a handle fashioned into the shape and colours of a freshwater trout. Utterly at home in the moors and in agricultural circles, he would have looked totally incongruous in a large town or city. Geoffrey was married to Marjorie who accompanied him to smart events such as hunt balls and important dinners, but she left the running of the estate to her competent husband.

It was during one of my routine motorbike patrols across the high moors which surrounded Wardle's estate that I paused to receive a radio transmission from Ashfordly Police Station. It was Alf Ventress.

'Control to Delta Alpha Two Four,' said Alf, using my call-sign.

Having halted, I picked up my handset and responded, 'Two Four to Control. Receiving, go ahead. Over.'

'Two Four. Location please.'

'Spindle Howe. Intended direction Brantsford, Stovensby and return to Ashfordly.'

'Received, Two Four. Please keep observations for a white Ford Escort DVN 767 C, stolen within the last half-hour at Eltering. If seen, do not intercept or interrogate the driver, but report direction and number of occupants. Over.'

'Received and understood. Two Four Out.'

'Control Out,' said Alf and so I jotted down the details in my notebook. The chances of the stolen vehicle crossing the remote moors where I was currently patrolling were very slim indeed, but I would keep my eyes open. The order not to stop the vehicle and interrogate the driver suggested the CID were anxious to trace this one—it had probably been involved in some other incident in Eltering, or the thief might be fleeing from a major crime elsewhere.

As I sat astride my bike, I decide to remain here for a while because my hilltop parking place presented an incredible 360° view. There are a few locations on the North York Moors which offer this kind of all-round vista, another being the moors close to Ralph Cross above Westerdale, but from where I was positioned I could look across to the North Sea to the east, the Wolds to the south, the never-ending panorama of heather to the north, and the villages of upper Ryedale to the west with the bulk of the Pennines in the far distance.

There was always a pair of high-powered binoculars in my panniers and so I lifted them out, adjusted them and began to range across the landscape below. I thought I might just catch sight of a fast-moving white Ford Escort if it was using any of the network of rural roads below me, but I did not see it. What I did see, however, was a completely bare hillside in the dale immediately to my right, i.e. about a mile to the south of my viewpoint. I had not previously seen it in that condition.

It was prominent because of its bald state—the other dales boasted steep sides that were covered with either conifers or heather, although some of the lower slopes comprised surprisingly lush grass meadows with dairy cattle. The bare hillside, known as Partridge Hill, formed part of the estate that belonged to Geoffrey Wardle, very remote and along an unmade track several miles from the big house and quite separate from the surrounding property. I thought nothing of the fact the hillside was bare—overall, the sight was not uncommon when the moorland was being cultivated.

Having spied on the countryside below me for several minutes, I decided to continue my patrol with one of my scheduled calls being at Stovensby. I had to take a statement from a lady who had witnessed a minor traffic accident in York—she had given her name and address to the injured pedestrian and so the police wanted her version of events. It took me about twenty-five minutes to drive down from the moors, through Brantsford and across the floor of the dale to Stovensby.

I parked my bike next to a Land Rover outside the post office and was collecting my file of statement forms from the panniers when Geoffrey Wardle emerged.

'By Jove, Constable,' he said cheerily. 'You nearly caught me red-handed . . . just been renewing my dog licence!'

'Good afternoon, sir,' I returned his greeting, as I walked towards the post office. 'Nice to know people around here are so law abiding!'

'That's what makes country life and country people so pleasant. So how's the world of crime around here?'

I told him about the car stolen from Eltering and then I decided to mention Partridge Hill.

'Oh, by the way, sir, I've just come down from the moors and while I was looking for that car, I noticed Partridge Hill's looking very bare—'

Before I could complete my sentence, he barked, 'Bare, you say? How do you mean, bare?' I could see the look of concern on his face.

'Well, as if your trees have been cut down . . . they were all so small, as I recall, and I thought it was odd—'

'Odd? It's more than bloody odd, Constable. Look, you'd better follow me . . . we'll go there right now. Without losing a moment.'

My interview with the witness was not particularly urgent and could be done later, so I agreed. He would lead me in his Land Rover and I would follow. He took me along some of his private roads, deep rutted and muddy, and along some surfaced lanes, then after half an hour or so he eased to a halt on the verge at the foot of Partridge Hill. I came to a stop behind him, hoisted the bike onto its rest and joined him.

'My God, Constable, just look at that . . . just you look at that . . . what a disaster . . . this is dreadful, really dreadful . . .'

As I looked at the ravaged hillside, all I could see was rough upturned earth amongst which were many deep holes and the scattered relics of plants such as briars, bracken, bits of heather and grass, along with many rocks. Mr Wardle just stood for a few moments in total silence then he said, 'Just look at it, Constable, just you look at it . . . all that hard work . . . gone.'

'Sir?' I was not sure how to react.

'Do you know what was here, Constable?'

'Young conifers, sir.'

'Yes, a crop of spruce, Constable. Small trees, they'd grown to about three feet tall . . . all of them . . . and now they've gone.'

'For Christmas trees, sir?'

'More than that, Constable. They're a major crop, the timber is used for all manner of things. Building work, pit props, packing cases, boxes of all types, paper-making and even in the manufacture of violins. A most versatile timber.'

'Are you saying they've been stolen, sir?'

'Yes, Constable, they have. Every one of them. Look at those holes—so they've not been cut down, they've been dug up and carried off, so they must have had transport, digging gear, time to work unhindered. Who would think anyone would steal an entire plantation of young spruce trees?'

'So how many are we talking about?'

'You're talking about seventeen hundred to two thousand trees per acre, planted so they've room to grow and to allow for losses . . . . and there's five acres here. They're thinned out after twenty years and mature between forty and seventy years. That's nearly ten thousand trees, Constable. Ten thousand! My investment—and the estate's—for the future.'

'So what would the thieves do with them?'

'They're no good for timber as they are, far too small and too young, and it's months until Christmas; the fact they've been uprooted suggests the thieves intend replanting them somewhere . . . they must have been stolen to order.'

'So when did they disappear?'

'Search me, Constable. I rarely travel out this way, there's never been the need. I'll have to ask my estate manager, gamekeeper and other staff.'

'I'll make a formal record of the crime, sir, I have the necessary forms in my panniers.'

'What's the point, Constable? How the hell can we get ten thousand trees back? And if we find them, how can I say they belong to me? I think it would be a waste of your time trying to find them.'

'Are you insured?'

'Well, we have a very comprehensive insurance through the estate, yes. You think it will cover theft of an entire plantation?'

'It's worth asking your insurers, sir. But if you do claim from them, they'll ask if you have reported it to the police, as a crime. You'll need to do that if the claim is to succeed.

We allocate a crime number to each reported crime and the insurance company will need that.'

'All right, Constable, you've persuaded me. Look, I need to find out more about this, when they were last seen in this plantation, for example, whether anyone's been seen around here with trucks and digging gear. Suppose you call in at the estate office tomorrow morning? I'll have everything ready for you, along with a valuation, when they were last seen, all you need to know.'

'Good, and that gives me time to speak to my sergeant. I know he will be concerned. What time would be convenient?'

'Eleven? For coffee?'

'Fine, sir.'

And so in due course I recorded the theft of approximately 10,000 young spruce trees worth about £83. Two pence per tree or so—it didn't sound a lot of money but that was their price at planting. What their price would be upon maturity in say, half a century's time, was guesswork, but it meant the estate had lost a considerable long-term investment.

We made extensive enquiries in the district and further afield, but no one had noticed any undue activity near Partridge Hill. The culprit or culprits were never traced, neither was Mr Wardle's crop of trees.

It was the only occasion within my experience when an entire plantation of trees was stolen. If they were replanted—probably the only thing that could usefully happen to them—they will be reaching maturity as these words are being read. And they will be worth much more than their original two old pennies per baby tree.

The stolen white Ford Escort was later found abandoned in Middlesbrough, but there was no reason to connect it or its thieves to the stolen plantation.

There is now a second plantation of steadily maturing spruces on Partridge Hill.

CHAPTER FOUR

One of my former training sergeants, addressing around thirty of us in a class of raw recruits during our initial training course, warned us that the way we dealt with certain incidents would help maintain and perpetuate the belief that the British police service was the finest in the world. He regarded that enduring public image as most important.

That particular sergeant, a dapper man who looked more like an optician than a policeman, clearly regarded the police service as a vocation rather than a mere job and he wanted everyone to have complete faith in it. That could only be achieved by the professionalism and good conduct of officers past and present. He exhorted us to remember that the whole of society should benefit from the actions of police officers.

During those early training sessions, therefore, it was impressed upon us that we should always deal with members of the public in a caring and humane manner. We were always to be polite and sincere, never lose our tempers or use bad language, always be smartly dressed both in uniform and in our civilian clothes, always be helpful and considerate and never over-bearing in the way we performed our duties or enforced the law.

'You can create an everlasting and very positive impression by the way you do your job,' he would repeatedly tell us during our lectures and practical sessions. 'Then, if you do make a good impression, the public will help and respect you—you and the entire police service will benefit.'

He went on to remind us that if we were to do our job properly when we left training school, we would need the willing co-operation and support of the general public. Without that, the police service could not function; it policed by consent.

'Yes, Sergeant,' we would chorus, fully intending to implement his teachings once we embarked on our first nerve-racking patrols in a police uniform.

'Remember, there are certain matters which place you in full critical view of the public—how you behave during those stressful moments will create a lasting impression. I ask that you remember that, and implore you to make an impact which is favourable and which reflects your professionalism.'

'Yes, Sergeant.'

'Now, these are some of the tasks that will determine how your actions are remembered—sudden or unexplained deaths, serious traffic accidents, informing someone that a relative or friend has died, domestic disputes and even routine things such as the way you perform point duty or enforce the traffic laws. In all those cases, you are in direct contact with the public in what is for them, a rather unpleasant or emotional situation. Remember you are allowed to use discretion in the way you enforce the law—without that, we would be living in a police state. Be flexible; don't impose the letter of the law on people; use tact and plenty of good humour. . . .'

'Yes, Sergeant.'

Our sergeant was very experienced and proud of the police service and it was inevitable that much of his enthusiasm and wise attitude rubbed off on most of us. With his missionary zeal in our minds, we left training school after three months' intensive tuition, and I think I speak for all recruits when I say we were determined to be good ambassadors for the service as we embarked on our varied, tough, testing and sometimes unexpected duties. Inevitably when we were posted to our first operational station to patrol the beat under a few weeks' protection of a fully experienced constable, we were surprised to be told, 'Forget whatever you were taught at training school—this is the real world.'

I ignored that cynicism because I accepted the sergeant's belief that much good could result from the way we constables performed our duties and so I went about my work with my training sergeant's vision of policing always in mind. There were times, though, when one might become disillusioned by the unwarranted and at times puzzling and hurtful behaviour of the great British public, even when it was involved with an emotional family concern such as a sudden death or serious traffic accident.

Such a case was the sudden and mysterious death of Sidney Henderson. I did not know Mr Henderson while he was alive for he did not live in Aidensfield; he was a resident of Shelvingby, one of the more remote villages on the moors above Ashfordly.

It was a fine, dry but cool November morning when I received a phone call from PC Alf Ventress. I was completing an hour's admin work in the office attached to my house at Aidensfield, my next task being to deliver those files to Ashfordly Police Station before embarking on my day's patrolling.

'Morning, Nick,' said Alf. 'Sorry to land you with this one but we've no one else available, they're all tied up with other jobs. It's a sudden death.'

'I've nothing pressing at the moment,' I admitted. 'So, yes, I'll attend to it, no problem. What's the story?'

'We've had a call from a hiker; he says there's a body in the river. A male, a pensioner by the look of him. Obviously dead. The body's just below where Shelvingby Beck joins the River Rye; there's a bridge and a footpath running beside the river. I've a map reference for you.'

'Right, thanks.'

He provided the necessary reference and before he rang off, I checked the location on the map that adorned one of my office walls, then said, 'I've found the location, Alf. I'll go straight away.'

'The caller will wait for you on the bridge, he's a Mr Kenneth Langton. He rang from the kiosk in Shelvingby.'

'I'll be there in twenty minutes.'

As I drove towards the scene, I saw on the arched stone bridge a middle-aged and sensibly clad hiker complete with rucksack and woolly hat. I parked the Mini-van and approached him.

'Mr Langton?'

'Yes, thanks for coming so quickly. He's dead, by the way, I told your office.'

'Yes, I received that information, thanks. Hence no ambulance. So what's the story? You can tell me as you guide me to the scene.'

As we walked, Mr Langton told me he was enjoying a solitary but late-season hiking holiday on the moors and was staying at a different bed-and-breakfast accommodation each night. This morning he'd set off early from Shelvingby, intending to take the riverside path to Ashfordly and then make for Eltering. He came from Leicester and provided me with his address and personal details, adding that it was something of a shock to make this gruesome discovery. With some first-aid knowledge, he had checked the body for signs of life, but found the unfortunate victim had been dead for some time.

After a ten minute walk along a very muddy and narrow path through trees displaying their last beautiful colours of autumn, we came to a clearing beside the river. The wooded banks opened onto a glade which, in summer, would be a small meadow full of flowers, low-lying with a tiny sandy beach, it bordered the banks of the river. It bore a line of debris, a reminder that the river had recently been in heavy flood.

'He's over there,' indicated Mr Langton.

I could see the body of a man lying face down half in the water and half on dry land; his head and torso were in the water with his legs spread-eagled across the modest sandy shore. As we approached, I could see he was dressed in corduroy trousers, walking boots and a dark sweater; he had thin grey hair with a bald patch on the crown of his head.

'Did you move him?' I asked Mr Langton, as we drew nearer.

'No, I just touched him on the cheek and checked his pulse, I think he's been dead a long time.'

'Was anyone else in the vicinity?'

'No, no one. There was no one to send for help so I had to leave him as I went to make my phone call. I didn't call the ambulance or doctor—no point, is there? He's beyond their help.'

'I'll just check for signs of injury while you're here,' I said. 'But from what I see, it looks as if he's drowned.'

I could not strip the corpse here to seek signs of physical injury, but could only carry out a visual examination—and that meant turning him over to see if there were stab wounds in his chest, bullet wounds in his head or some other indication of violence which might turn this into a murder investigation. The only marks of violence were on his face, but I thought these might have occurred after death, as his body had been carried downstream and battered against underwater rocks or obstructions. There was no sign of blood—but dead bodies did not bleed.

'He looks like a hiker. Have you come across him anywhere?'

'No, I can't say I know him.'

'Hmm. It looks as though he's fallen in and drowned,' I said, adding, 'but I'm not qualified to make that kind of decision. I'll have to call the police doctor to examine him before we move him, and to certify death. Because the death is mysterious, and if the doctor cannot give a cause of death, there'll have to be a post-mortem and perhaps an inquest.

Once I've taken a written statement from you I can let you go, Mr Langton, but if there is an inquest you might be asked to give evidence about finding him.'

'I understand.'

'Now, before I return to my van to call the doctor, I need to see if there are any documents of identification on him.'

I searched his wet pockets and among a few personal belongings such as his handkerchief, pen-knife, a few pence in coppers, a ball point pen and a hair comb, I found a leather wallet containing a couple of soggy pound notes and a driving licence in the name of Sidney Henderson, Spring Cottage, Shelvingby. There was also a Yale key tucked into a pocket of the wallet. I told Mr Langton that it seemed he was a local man who had had an unfortunate accident and said I would later inform him of the outcome of the post-mortem and my enquiries. I made a note in my pocket book that I had found the wallet and taken temporary possession of it in my efforts to identify the deceased and trace his relatives. Eventually, it would be placed with his other personal belongings.

Although Mr Langton had been delayed for about an hour due to finding the body, he walked back to the bridge with me and I then took the necessary formal written statement on forms kept in my van. I allowed him to remain with me as I radioed Ashfordly Police Station to set in motion the procedures that surrounded a sudden or mysterious death. I thought he would like to know that our response was both positive and immediate.

As he disappeared to complete his schedule for that day, I waited beside my van which was parked a short distance from the bridge, and then Dr William Williams of Ashfordly arrived. A burly and fiery Welshman, he asked for my account of events to date as I escorted him to the scene. I knew that Harold Poulter, the Ashfordly undertaker, would have been called out by Alf and he would arrive soon. He would have in his vehicle the shell, a plastic, coffin-shaped container used for shifting bodies to the mortuary and so the business of the day began in earnest.

Dr Williams commenced his examination and then, after a few minutes, looked at the man's face and said, 'I know this gentleman, PC Rhea, he's a patient of mine. Sidney Henderson from Shelvingby, long sufferer from heart problems. In his seventies. I'd say he died from a heart attack, but we'll have to wait for the pathologist to confirm that. So all you need is for me to confirm he's dead, right?'

'Thank you, yes, that's if you can't confirm the cause of death?'

'I can't, no, not under these circumstances. Opinion yes, confirmation, no. After all, he might have drowned.'

A brief but skilled examination of the body then followed after which Dr Williams, for legal purposes, confirmed the fellow was dead. He added the body had been dead for a considerable time but would not hazard a guess as to precisely how long. 'At least a day, maybe two,' was all he would say. He confirmed there were no outward signs of violence other than those apparently caused to the face, by the body probably being carried downstream in heavy water. He stressed he could not conduct a full examination of the body without undressing it—but that would be done during the post-mortem by the pathologist.

'He lived alone, you know,' said Dr Williams, as he prepared to leave. 'He should have had his wife and family to care for him, but he had no one. Sad really; he was a very nice man. Used to have a shop in Scarborough, a successful businessman.'

I thanked Dr Williams who then left to go about his rounds in Ashfordly and district. When Harold Poulter arrived, the body would be taken to Ashfordly General Hospital for the necessary post-mortem examination. Ambulances were not used for the transport of dead bodies—they were for the living or those who might die *en route* to hospital. Harold's old hearse (not his splendidly polished modern one) would be eminently suitable. When Harold arrived, I accompanied the body to the mortuary and provisionally identified it to the pathologist as Sidney Henderson, even though we did not have official confirmation—this was sufficient to set in motion the various official procedures. And so my investigation into the death of Sidney Henderson got underway.

Having overseen the removal of his mortal remains to a place more suited to visitors who might wish to view his body, I now had to pass the sad news to Mr Henderson's relatives. Whenever possible, this difficult and sensitive task was always done in person rather than by telephone, and in cases of sudden or unexplained deaths, it was preferable that the police officer in charge of the enquiries performed that essential duty. It established a firm link between the relatives, the police and the investigation, always a harrowing time for everyone involved. This was the kind of delicate personal duty mentioned by that old training sergeant and I recalled his advice. I had to treat the relatives with tenderness and care.

Keen to get the task finished, I radioed Alf Ventress from the car park at Ashfordly Hospital, told him I was sure the deceased was Sidney Henderson with an address in Shelvingby, and that I was now heading to that village to inform his next-of-kin. I added that, to date, the death did not seem suspicious—it had all the appearances of an accident. Nonetheless, we both knew that much depended upon the post-mortem result; if, as a result of his examination, the pathologist had any concerns about the cause of death such as poisoning, the effect of drugs or other suspicious means, he would seek the necessary expert advice.

Shelvingby is a very small moorland village perched on the steep hillside with magnificent views over the surrounding moorland and dale.

Its tiny cluster of houses are all sturdily built of local stone with blue slate roofs and, when viewed from a distance, they look like dolls' houses clinging together among the heather for support and shelter from the bleak moorland weather. There is a large house known as Shelvingby Hall, the Black Lion inn, a tiny parish church in the dale below, and a modest shop-cum-post office that occupies the living-room of its owner's cottage. The total population is probably less than a hundred although the village is always popular with tourists, day trippers and visitors.

As I did not know which was Mr Henderson's cottage, I popped into the shop and spoke to the proprietor, Mrs Hollins. A matronly lady in her mid-fifties, she knew everyone and everything that happened in Shelvingby.

'It's that cottage by the beck, Mr Rhea,' she told me. 'Just over the bridge and a couple of hundred yards along to your right. Small place, a bit overgrown with rubbish now, it needs a lick of paint. Is he all right? I'm asking because he wasn't around this morning when I took his paper. His fire's usually on and he's generally in the kitchen, doing his breakfast. In fact, I haven't seen him for a day or two. He usually pops in when he's out and about in the village.'

'Well, I'm afraid this is bad news.' I decided I could tell her—it would soon be common knowledge anyway and his relatives were my next call. 'He was found dead this morning, down by the river. I think it might be a heart attack. I'm here to tell his relatives.'

'Oh dear; I thought it funny when he wasn't around these last few days. Poor Mr Henderson, he was so lonely, you know . . . but relatives? What relatives?'

'Well, I thought he must have a wife or someone, children perhaps?'

'He has, Mr Rhea, but they never come anywhere near him, not them! Even when he was in hospital with his heart they never visited. He might as well not exist. They never come to see him and he's never invited to call on them. He lives alone, always has, ever since coming to live here.'

'So where do his relations live?'

'His wife's in Chester, I think—don't ask me her address—and he has two sons, both living somewhere down south. With families. His grandchildren. He's never divorced his wife, she just left him.'

'Really? That's odd. Anyway, I'm going to the house next, I think I have the right key. If I can't find any addresses there, I'll get the local police to try and find Mrs Henderson; she'll be in the electoral register. Is there anyone who will look after the house until all this gets sorted out?'

'Yes, Mr Jacobs next door—they were good pals. He'll have a spare key; he's always kept one in case anything happened to Sidney.'

I found Mr Jacob's cottage. He was clearly a pensioner and he was busy in his garden, clearing away dead plants. I hailed him. The moment he saw me, I could see the expression of alarm on his face.

'Is it about Sidney?' he asked. 'I guessed something was wrong, with him not being around these last few days.'

'Yes, I'm sorry to bring bad news.' I introduced myself and explained. He listened carefully as I told him what had happened, and what would now happen to Sidney during the next few days.

'Oh dear, oh dear, the poor man. He did have heart problems, you know, but liked walking. Not that he was a hiker or long-distance enthusiast. He just liked the fresh air and exercise. Although he knew the risks, he wouldn't give up his walking . . . it gave him something to live for.'

'I need to get into his house, Mr Jacobs, to see if I can locate his relatives. I understand he lived alone.'

'Yes, and I have a key. Shall I get it for you?'

'Well, I have one. I have his wallet. I needed that to obtain his name and address for a provisional identification,' and I showed him the Yale.

'Yes, that's for the front door.'

'Thanks. Well, I'll see if I can find his address book, but I don't want anything else. I'll lock up and let you know when I'm leaving.'

The cottage was extremely small with only a kitchen and a living-room downstairs, one bedroom and a bathroom upstairs, and an outside toilet in a tiny yard at the rear. I had no difficulty finding the telephone with Mr Henderson's address book beside it. I checked it under the 'Henderson' name and found an address in Chester for Carol. His wife?

Also, I found two more addresses under that name—Andrew Henderson and Jonathan Henderson, with what I guessed were the names of their wives and children.

I jotted the names in my notebook because I thought Mr Jacobs might have need of the address book, and then left. I would ask the local police to contact each of those relations to inform them of his death, and to ask at least one of them to come to Yorkshire to arrange the funeral. I secured the cottage and told Mr Jacobs what I had done, and then asked if he would be willing to look at the body in the mortuary to confirm my provisional identification. The name I had found could not be accepted as a legal finality—he could have had someone else's wallet in his possession, but my effort had allowed the preliminary procedures to begin. Clearly, Mr Jacobs knew Henderson very well and he agreed. Without delay, I drove him to the hospital where I led him into the mortuary; Henderson's remains were on a slab and covered with a white sheet and so I pulled back the sheet to show the face.

'Is that the man you know as Sidney Henderson of Spring Cottage, Shelvingby?' I asked the necessary question and he replied simply, 'Yes, that's him.' This provided the necessary confirmation and so I got him to sign a short statement to that effect in my notebook—now the post-mortem could proceed. It meant that we did not have to await the arrival of his wife or other relations for an official identification—that would be necessary later. I then returned Mr Jacobs to his house and motored down to Ashfordly Police Station to update Alf Ventress and Sergeant Craddock. The sergeant was now in his office and so I gave him a full account of my morning's efforts so far.

'What time is the post-mortem?' he asked.

Alf responded on my behalf. 'Three this afternoon, Sergeant. It's the earliest they could fit us in. And the coroner has been informed, he's awaiting the outcome of the post-mortem too.'

'Good, well, that will determine our next action. So what are you doing next, PC Rhea?'

'I'm going to get the local police to go around to Mrs Henderson and their two sons, to tell them of his death.'

'Don't forget to get one of the next-of-kin to come here as soon as possible—we've got him identified sufficiently for our immediate purposes, but there's still the funeral to arrange and we'll need legal proof of his identity. And I am sure there'll be family matters to sort out.'

And so I set about making my telephone calls to the respective police forces, leaving my Aidensfield number and that of Ashfordly Police Station as contact points, had lunch and then went to the post-mortem. As the Coroner's Officer for this particular sudden death, and because of the continuity of evidence, I had to attend. In the North Riding Constabulary, the officer dealing with any sudden death was automatically the Coroner's Officer for the duration of the enquiry into that death; in city and borough forces, however, where the population was greater, there was usually a full-time Coroner's Officer.

Prior to being posted to Aidensfield, and during my service there, I had attended many post-mortems and had no qualms watching the pathologist cut open the body and examine various organs, but his findings were straightforward if a little surprising.

'He did not die from drowning, PC Rhea, I can tell you that because there is no water in his lungs, neither has he clutched at underwater plants and weeds in his death throes. He was dead before he entered the water. He had a recurring heart problem—his heart and arteries are in a very poor condition and in simple language that caused his death. In other words, he died from natural causes. How he got into the water is not for me to determine, but in my opinion he collapsed and fell in, perhaps from the bridge upstream or from the riverbank. The condition of his clothing and the water-borne debris in his clothes suggests he was in the water for some time, and the facial injuries indicate his body was carried a distance downriver to be swept ashore where you found it. Those injuries occurred after death, by the way, he was not the victim of a beating or assault of any kind. Those sorts of injuries are possible bearing in mind we had floods in recent days. I will compile my formal report for your office and for the coroner.'

I returned to the police station in Ashfordly to complete my own report, and then it was time to go home. The body would remain in the mortuary, and in custody of the coroner, until the coroner issued his authority to bury the remains—the so-called Pink Form. Then the remains would be returned to the care of the next-of-kin so that the funeral could proceed and other legal formalities completed.

It had been a busy day but interesting and then, just as I was sitting down to my tea with Mary and the children, the phone rang. It was Cheshire Police.

'Ah, PC Rhea, this is the Enquiry Office at Chester sub-division. I am PC Finnegan. I have to report I visited Mrs Carol Henderson in accordance with your request message, but she has asked me to inform you she wants nothing to do with her husband. She will not be coming to his home, nor will she be arranging his funeral. And neither will her sons. She wanted you to be quite clear about that. She made it a very clear statement that she wants nothing to do with him, dead or alive.'

For a few moments I was stunned by this response, and then managed to ask, 'Did she give any reason?'

'No,' he said. 'Nothing.'

'They're not divorced, are they?'

'No, she mentioned that. They have lived apart for about thirty years she told me, but she has never divorced him.'

'Is she a Catholic?' I asked. 'They don't believe in divorce.'

'No idea, sorry,' he said.

'Well, thanks for delivering the message. Now we have a problem about who's going to identify him formally for issue of the death certificate, and who's going to bury him.'

'I'm sure you'll sort something out! Sorry I can't be more helpful.'

After obtaining Mrs Henderson's address and telephone number in case I, or anyone else, needed to contact her, I put down the handset but thought I would sleep on this one until tomorrow, then I would pass the somewhat disturbing news to Sergeant Craddock. So who would attend to Mr Henderson's house and belongings, or arrange his funeral?

'Are you coming for your tea or not?' Mary shouted through to my office. 'It's getting cold!'

'On my way,' I responded.

I drove into Ashfordly Police Station next morning for a meeting with Sergeant Craddock about disposal of Mr Henderson's body once the Pink Form was issued. There was also the question of the disposal of the house and its contents. Sergeant Craddock said that was not the concern of the police, but we did need to get the business of disposal of the body sorted out.

'There is a procedure for this kind of situation.' Craddock had his office copy of *Moriarty's Police Law* open on his desk. 'Listen to this,' he said. '"Councils of county boroughs and county districts shall cause to be buried or cremated the body of any person who has died or been found dead in their area in any case where no suitable arrangements for the disposal of the body have been or are being made otherwise than by the council." That is laid down in the National Assistance Act of 1948, section 50.'

'A pauper's burial, you mean?'

'I'm afraid so—that's the only way unless someone comes forward to take responsibility. I'll start the ball rolling today. I'll ring the council to alert them to this one and I'm sure they'll contact Mrs Henderson, just to make sure she or her sons still refuse to bury him. Meanwhile, I think you should return to the village and ask around to see if anyone has been looking after the old chap. He must have friends and neighbours. There might be someone who will organize the funeral; maybe he's arranged a power of attorney or left a will, and we need his birth certificate to prove his age. Who owns his house, for example? Is it rented, and does he have a bank account? Get yourself up to Shelvingby, PC Rhea, have a look through his personal belongings and do a spot of detective work—we need to know as much as we can about this peculiar situation.'

When I returned to Shelvingby, my first call was upon Mr Jacobs.

He took me into his pretty cottage where his wife, Amy, produced a pot of tea and some biscuits, and then we chatted about Sidney Henderson. I explained the situation and both were horrified at the thought of him suffering a pauper's funeral. Jacobs suggested he might organize the funeral, but I reminded him that it could be costly, and without access to Mr Henderson's bank account, it would not be possible to use his money.

'So does that mean his wife will inherit his savings? And this house and contents?'

'Unless he's made a will to the contrary, yes,' I admitted. 'But if the council bury him, they will pay the costs but they will not see to the disposal of the house and contents, especially as his wife and children are still alive. They are the automatic inheritors of his estate unless he has made a will to the contrary.'

'That is despicable!' fumed Mr Jacobs. 'She's bled him dry all these years . . . refused to get a divorce to force him into supporting her and her sons. She left him, Mr Rhea. He did not leave her but he has paid and paid all through those long years and now she won't give him a decent burial and will get her share of his estate. I don't know how she can live with her conscience or how she copes with that kind of mentality.'

'Clearly, he talked to you?'

'Yes, I was his best friend, Mr Rhea. He was a lovely man, so kind and unassuming, a true friend. Everyone in Shelvingby liked him.'

'So did he appoint a power of attorney?'

'Not to my knowledge. I don't think he made a will either. If he had, I am sure I would have been asked to witness his signature, but nothing like that has ever happened. Whatever he has will go to his wife and sons, that is not really our concern, but he does deserve a decent funeral. Really, I think I should do something about it.'

'Well, I won't press you into doing it, although I suppose you could get the undertaker to send his bill to the wife. But meanwhile I must search his house—I need things like his birth certificate, any will he might have made, details of his bank and so forth.'

'It's all there, Mr Rhea; he has a small bureau in his front room and he kept all his personal stuff in it. He once told me that if he died, I would find everything in there.'

'Thanks, I'll go and have a look. I'll make a list of the things I take away and will let you know what they are. And, finally, do you have any idea why his wife left him like his, and never divorced him?'

'No, no idea, Mr Rhea. She wasn't a Catholic and neither was he so it's nothing to do with religion. She never sought a divorce and so he kept paying towards her upkeep and that of her sons . . . a dutiful father he was.'

'And the sons never came to visit him either?'

'No, no one. He has no brothers or sisters either, he is—er, was—very much on his own. But the village liked him; he was a very nice man and a good neighbour, helpful with village activities, supportive of events we organized . . . he liked it here, and we liked him. You know, the more I talk to you, the more I realize I should arrange his funeral, PC Rhea, I really should. And I will see if I can get support from the village. There's no way the people of Shelvingby can allow Sidney to have a pauper's funeral.'

'I find it odd that his wife left him without divorcing him.'

'Everyone felt the same, Mr Rhea. But Sidney never talked about it and I never heard him complain about her either. He told us very little about his working life, except he once had a shop in Scarborough, and owned a few flats he let to holidaymakers. That helped him eke out his pension, he once told me. Actually, he will be worth quite a lot of money, Mr Rhea, he still owned those holiday flats, a small block of six.'

Mrs Jacobs confirmed her husband's account and supported his opinion of Sidney Henderson; so, after talking to them at length, I felt I had gained a clear impression of him. Next, I went to his house and let myself in. In some ways, I felt like a trespasser but I reconciled my intrusion by telling myself I was doing this for Sidney Henderson—already, I felt he would not tolerate a pauper's funeral—and I wondered what else his home would reveal. Home is where one's secrets are kept—and hidden.

It was easy to locate his personal documents. Having owned a shop, he dealt with his personal correspondence in a simple but efficient way and, as Mr Jacobs had said, everything was kept in the bureau in his living-room. Quite soon, I found his birth certificate but no wedding certificate (I guessed his wife had taken custody of that). I also found details of his bank accounts, one being personal and the other business—he still had an income from his letting properties and this was administered by an estate agent who deducted his fees before passing the cheques on to Mr Henderson. I found three building society passbooks, his post office savings account, old age pension book, showing he was seventy-five years old, house deeds, private pension documents, electricity and telephone accounts, rate bills, water rates and all the normal outgoings for a small household of this kind. His bank statements recorded his outgoings and I noted he had a standing order for monthly payments of £120 to Mrs Henderson's bank account in Chester. His address book, which I had earlier examined, was also there. Although I had no authority to seize these personal documents, I decided I would take them into safekeeping at the police station, to be added to his other personal items. They would be safer there than left in the empty house because some of his building society passbooks contained substantial sums of money. I made a list of everything I took, locked the house and went to see Mr Jacobs to explain what I had done. I told him that if, for any reason he required sight of these papers, they would be at the police station in Ashfordly unless restored to Mr Henderson's next-of-kin. I also asked Mr Jacobs to keep either me or Sergeant Craddock informed if he or the village community decided to arrange the funeral. I gave him Harold Poulter's address and said he had already carried out some work on behalf of Mr Henderson's family—he had moved his remains from the riverside although those costs would be paid by the coroner.

When I returned to the police station to deliver Mr Henderson's documents, I learned that the coroner had issued his Pink Form which meant the funeral could go ahead without the need for an inquest. In effect, that marked the end of the police investigation. Without holding an inquest, the coroner was satisfied that the death of Mr Sidney Henderson was due to natural causes although how he had got into the river was never determined. The pathologist's theory was the most logical.

We learned later from Mr Jacobs that Shelvingby village community had decided to fund Mr Henderson's funeral in their tiny parish church, to be followed by a funeral tea in the village hall; if every family shared the cost, their individual and personal contributions would be minimal and so he would be spared the indignity of a pauper's burial. I decided I would attend, albeit wondering how his house, flats and personal belongings would be disposed of. The funeral was held five days after his death, and it was a moving occasion with the church full of villagers and a pleasing tribute from the vicar—but no family members.

It would be a few days later when I chanced to be in Ashfordly Police Station when Alf Ventress received a phone call from a firm of solicitors in Chester. Alf passed the phone to me.

'It's some solicitors from Chester,' he said. 'About Mr Henderson's death.'

'PC Rhea,' I announced myself. 'How can I help you?'

'My name is Nesbitt,' said the male voice. 'I am representing Mrs Carol Henderson whose husband died recently in Shelvingby.'

'Good afternoon, Mr Nesbitt. How can I help? I dealt with the sudden death of Mr Henderson.'

'Can I ask whether the funeral has taken place? And whether there was an inquest?'

'Yes it has taken place. The post-mortem examination showed Mr Henderson had died from natural causes, a heart attack in simple terms, and it appears he fell into the river. A sad end. There was no inquest. The villagers clubbed together to prevent a pauper's burial, he now lies peacefully in Shelvingby church yard.'

'Ah good. Now, Mr Henderson's wife and sons are, of course, entitled to his estate even if he died intestate and so, in order to finalize matters and deal with the inheritance, I need access to his personal documents, house deeds, bank accounts and so forth. Where can I find those?'

'All his personal documents and official papers are in Ashfordly Police Station, Mr Nesbitt, awaiting collection by someone with the appropriate authority. We put them there for safekeeping. The house is standing empty, except for its furnishings of course, and the key is also with his papers. A Mr Jacobs in Shelvingby has another key—he is caring for the house and we are keeping an eye on it during our routine patrols.'

'Excellent news. I am sure Mrs Henderson will appreciate what you have done, and perhaps she will write you a letter of thanks. Now, it is my intention to travel across to Yorkshire, probably next Tuesday, so will that be convenient to collect the papers? Say eleven o'clock?'

'Yes, Ashfordly Police Station is always staffed. I'll leave a note for the sergeant to advise him to expect you.'

'Good, and afterwards I shall visit the house in Shelvingby with a local estate agent and we shall arrange its clearance and sale of the contents, then put it on the market. Mrs Henderson wants to dispose of it, and some properties in

Scarborough, at the earliest opportunity. Then we can forget all about Sidney Henderson.'

'As you wish,' was all I could think of saying.

And that, finally, was the end of my involvement with the sudden death of Sidney Henderson. Throughout my enquiries, everyone said what a lovely person he was, how kind and thoughtful, and what an asset he was to a small moorland community like Shelvingby. None could throw any light on the behaviour of his wife and family, but in spite of their long-term separation from him and their lack of remorse at his death, they would inherit everything which when added together was worth a considerable sum. It all seemed so unfair and unreasonable on her part, but it appeared that, over the years, she had been deliberately forcing him to pay her, perhaps for some misdemeanour he had committed in the distant past? Had he had an affair? Did she know some kind of secret which he did not wish to be revealed? Was her action a subtle kind of domestic blackmail?

It was a few months later when, by chance and quite unrelated to Mr Henderson's death, I received a telephone call from the secretary of the North Riding branch of NARPO, the National Association for Retired Police Officers.

'Nick,' it was Arthur Edwards calling. 'Nick, ex-Detective Sergeant Ron Richards lives on your patch, doesn't he?'

'Yes,' I confirmed. 'In Elsinby. A few doors from the Hopbind Inn.'

'Look, we've not heard from him recently. I've sent him the usual mail from NARPO but he hasn't responded, and he didn't cash his last pension cheque. He's not on the phone so I can't ring him. I'm wondering if he's got a problem of some kind. Can you check for me?'

'Sure,' I said. 'I think I'd have known if he was having difficulties, but yes, Arthur, I'll go this morning. I'll call you back later today.'

NARPO was the welfare association for police pensioners, overseeing matters like their pensions but also checking on their personal circumstances and welfare in retirement.

There is a branch in every police force, staffed by retired officers working on a voluntary basis.

When I arrived at Ron's semi-detached house, I could see someone was at home because smoke was rising from the chimney and so I went to the back door and knocked. He answered almost immediately.

'Oh, Nick, hello. Come in. I was in the kitchen, making myself a coffee. Do you fancy one?'

Ron Richards was a sturdy man now in his middle sixties but he sported a head of thick grey hair and always looked fit and strong. His wife had died some six years earlier, but he was settled in Elsinby where his neighbours kept an eye on him, and where his son and two daughters were regular visitors.

He frequented the Hopbind Inn where he could obtain meals if he didn't fancy cooking for himself and indeed the landlady, Sally Ward, would always keep any leftovers for him, especially if she'd had a large group to cater for. With a large group, there was always something spare. Without asking why I had called on duty, he led me into his neat living-room where the fire was blazing and bade me sit down. Like most retired policemen, Ron was always pleased to hear news of the service and of his former colleagues. I updated him as best I could, and then he asked, 'So, Nick, what brings you here?'

'I had a call from NARPO,' I told him. 'Arthur Edwards said he hadn't heard from you recently and he wondered if you were all right.'

'That's good of him; it's nice to know somebody cares!' laughed Ron. 'But yes, Nick, I'm fine. Never felt better, in fact. Mind, I had a bit of a wobbly a week or two ago, dizzy spells. My age, I think, so my younger daughter, Alison, took me to her house for a couple of weeks. She reckoned I needed a rest! I do nothing but rest these days! Anyway, I went and just got back the day before yesterday. I've been to the quack and he says my heart's alright, so, as I said earlier, I'm as fit as a fiddle. But thank Arthur, won't you? It is reassuring to know he's keeping an eye on me.'

We chatted about events and personalities in the force with him reminiscing about the good old days, as ex-policemen are prone to do, and then I decided to ask about Sidney Henderson—Ron had been a young detective in Scarborough around the time Sidney would have had his shop.

I told Ron about Sidney's sudden death and the strange behaviour of his wife.

'I remember him,' said Ron. 'He had a sweet shop—a good one on the sea front, very busy especially in summer selling sticks of Scarborough rock. Then there was an almighty rumpus. Somebody accused him of interfering with little girls, taking them into the back room of his shop and behaving indecently in return for free sweets. Rumours spread like wildfire, as they do in such cases, and we got ourselves involved. We interviewed dozens of kids, boys and girls, but never found a shred of evidence against him. They all liked Sidney; he was a typical sweet-shop owner, chatty and kind to everyone. It was one of those difficult crimes—so easy to make an allegation but so difficult to prove one's innocence.'

'So what was your opinion?'

'I thought he was completely innocent, and so did my colleagues. But the local paper got hold of the story and that was enough—even though his name was never mentioned, people turned their backs on poor old Sidney. His wife left him while threatening to make him pay for the rest of his life, and all the parents kept their kids away from his shop. He sold up and went to live in the country. But there was no prosecution and not a shred of evidence against him.'

'Poor chap.'

'He was a shrewd businessman, Nick. When he was making a few bob, he invested in some holiday flats and they kept him solvent, and I'm sure that in his rural retreat, he would find a way of earning a few quid.'

'His wife refused to bury him,' I said.

'She was a bitch of the highest order, Nick. At the very time he needed support from his family, his wife especially, she left him—and she's been bleeding him dry ever since. Call it blackmail if you will—but if anyone should have known of his innocence, it should have been her.'

'Maybe he wasn't as innocent as we think?'

'Who knows, Nick? All we coppers can do is go on the evidence and there was none to convict him. Not a scrap.'

'The people of Shelvingby liked him,' I said. 'They organized his funeral, and paid for it.'

'I wonder what they would have done if they'd known about those rumours?' he asked. 'His wife would never reveal them—that's why she went to live a long way off. She didn't want folks to know about her husband and his link with that scandal—it would reflect too much on her if they'd been true, and so his secret—if that's what it was—has gone to the grave with him.'

'And his wife has gained financial benefit from him, even after death.'

'Hell hath no fury, and all that!' he sighed.

CHAPTER FIVE

The unusual circumstances surrounding the sudden death of Sidney Henderson did not permit me to demonstrate to his relatives the professionalism and caring attitude of either myself or the police service as a whole. They took no part whatever in those sad proceedings and in fact it was his friends and neighbours in the tiny community of Shelvingby who showed compassion for him. However, as my old training sergeant had told my class of fellow recruits all those years earlier, there would be many other incidents and occasions in which the constabulary and its members could shine. I recalled him saying that among them, traffic accidents, particularly those involving personal injuries, demanded high standards of professional care from the officers who dealt with them.

Much depends upon the actions of the first officer at the scene of an accident, then known in police jargon as an RTA (road traffic accident). In any motor accident, however minor, there is always an element of shock and bewilderment especially during the first few minutes. In the immediate aftermath, no one is quite certain what do to; no one is utterly sure what happened and the first worry of most drivers or victims is to wonder whether they are personally responsible. There is always the risk of unrecognized internal personal injuries too and in almost every accident there is expensive damage to one's precious motor vehicle. At times, one or other of the parties involved can explode into fits of anger and recrimination, or collapse in tears or even flee from the scene. It is traumatic for all concerned.

In addition there is always the risk of further accidents with the likelihood of speeding vehicles careering into those already involved. This is particularly the case on major roads, motorways, narrow country roads with sharp corners and, of course, during conditions of ice, fog or snow. Those first moments following an RTA are the most dangerous and harrowing time for all, even for those police, ambulance, fire brigade and medical personnel who attend to sort out the mess. In addition to dealing with the injured or shocked, they must prevent further accidents which can, at times, put police officers or other emergency services in real danger. Quite often, once the situation has been finalized, those involved in the accident, even in a minor capacity, will write letters of thanks to the police and other emergency services who dealt with them so sympathetically even at times when a prosecution may follow.

During my time at Aidensfield, road traffic accidents formed a substantial proportion of my daily routine. In police terms, most were very ordinary and unexceptional, generally involving two vehicles in some form of minor collision on junctions, crossroads and narrow minor routes. I dealt with accidents involving cars, lorries, vans, buses, motorbikes, cyclists, pedestrians, tractors, combine harvesters, steam rollers and even ancient and antique cars. Some resulted in prosecutions for careless driving or perhaps for not having a valid tax disc, driving licence or third party insurance and all were fed into the statistics department at force headquarters who could then determine the danger points on local roads.

Coloured stickers were placed on a large map of the county and each indicated a particular type of accident, i.e. one involving a pedestrian, an animal, a single-vehicle accident, service bus and so forth. The accidents were also graded such as fatal, serious or slight. Over a period of years, therefore, or even months, the sites at which frequent accidents occurred could be readily identified if lots of stickers accumulated in one place. Steps would then be taken to upgrade the road, remove a dangerous bend, erect warning signs of crossroads and junctions, install a pedestrian crossing or generally make the road safer for all in whatever way necessary. Whenever a fatal accident occurred, it was highlighted on the map with a black sticker, hence the term 'accident black spot', especially when several such accidents occurred at the same location. That kind of evidence usually indicated a fault with the road layout rather than a fault with drivers.

That map, useful though it was for introducing road safety measures, could not indicate the trauma which was involved in any of the accidents depicted upon it. Even the loss of a pet dog or cat is harrowing (although accidents to cats and wild animals were not recorded) and coping with the aftermath of a serious accident was often left to family members and friends whether or not it involved a court appearance for one or other of the drivers involved. Sometimes medical experts were asked to treat the victims even if no injury was immediately apparent and for that reason, shock was eventually recognized as an 'injury' for road safety statistical purposes. The effects of severe shock could be serious and might endure for a long period after a serious accident.

It was against this general background that we police officers went about our daily routine in the full knowledge that we could be expected to deal with an RTA on an average of once a week, even in a quiet area. On the busier roads, that figure could rise to several per day, hence the formation of the specialist Road Traffic Division in every police force, but in the calm of rural Aidensfield and district, I was not unduly overburdened with traffic accidents even though they were a dominant feature of my work. Many of the very minor ones were never reported but, of course, whenever an accident did happen, it was always unexpected. That meant it required immediate action. That was one of the requisites of police duty—so much of our work demanded an instant response.

One of the main weapons in the British road safety system is the driving test which, so we are led to believe, equips ordinary mortals with all the skills necessary to safely propel a motor vehicle along our increasingly congested roads. There are different tests for different categories of vehicle such as cars, cars with trailers, a range of buses, various sizes of commercial vehicles with or without trailers, along with mopeds and motorcycles, agricultural vehicles, road rollers, tracked vehicles and more. In the 1960s, however, it was usually professional drivers who needed specialist licences; most ordinary people were content to pass the required test to drive either a motorcycle or a motor car.

That era was also the time when more and more women were obtaining driving licences—I think it is fair to say that before World War II, comparatively few women were qualified drivers. There were some, of course. Many could drive cars long before driving licences and driving tests were introduced and later many worked as drivers in HM Forces during the war. Nonetheless, women drivers were rare in some places and I can recall, in my childhood, the time I first saw a woman at the wheel of a car. It was during the 1940s and was one of those occasions one remembers for the rest of one's life, like learning that the war was over, or that President Kennedy had been shot. Now, of course, it is not in the least unusual to see a woman driving any kind of motor vehicle.

It was perhaps that prevailing pre-war attitude that prevented Freda Holden from even considering she might drive a car or pass a driving test. Freda and her husband, Godfrey, lived at No. 6, Howe End Cottages, Elsinby. Both were retired, having owned and run a fruit and vegetable shop in York. It had been a very successful business, with Freda looking after the accounts and other admin work, including the ordering, while Godfrey served in the shop and undertook regular deliveries across York and district in his small green van. Freda could not drive, consequently she never made those deliveries.

Whenever her husband was out on his rounds, Freda would take over at the counter and it was generally accepted they were a loving couple who made ideal and trustworthy shopkeepers.

Their long-term customers included some of York's finest hotels and catering establishments. As he headed for retirement age though, Godfrey began to suffer from high blood pressure and then heart problems. Freda's health remained good so they decided that Godfrey should remain in business until he reached retirement age (provided his health permitted), and then they would sell their business along with their York home, and live in retirement at Elsinby.

That was Freda's childhood village and it had long been her ambition to retire there; Godfrey, although a townsman, had no objections and seemed willing to adapt to country life. After all, Freda had supported him during his working life and so he would try to please her in their well-earned retirement. He managed to reach retirement age while still in business although he was taking things much easier at that point. The style and reputation of his business remained very positive and it sold easily. Their two children, Graham and Jessica, supported the couple in their move to the North Yorkshire countryside although Graham, who worked for Rowntree's chocolate factory in York, cautiously suggested his mum should learn to drive.

'Dad's health isn't too good,' he reminded her on several occasions. 'If anything happens to him, you'll be stuck out there in the sticks. There's no buses or trains in Elsinby, remember, so you'll need a car.'

'A car's no good to me!' she said, with a degree of stubbornness. 'I can't drive; besides your dad can still drive. And I was born in Elsinby; we didn't have cars then and it wasn't a problem.'

As they settled into country life, they were blissfully happy in Elsinby, going for long walks around the village, becoming involved with local organizations, patronizing the Hopbind Inn and generally finding themselves both accepted and liked, a rare thing for some incomers. There were those who came to live in such a village and then promptly tried to urbanize the place by suggesting street lights, pedestrian crossings, parking restrictions and other townish ideas. Godfrey and Freda did no such thing—they were far too wise.

But even in the relaxed atmosphere of retirement, Godfrey's health did not improve. His heart continued to cause concern and Dr Archie McGee told him to rest—he even recommended a couple of weeks in St Aidan's Cottage Hospital in Elsinby to enforce a period of absolute rest and calm with none of the worries about running his household and tending the garden.

It was Godfrey's deteriorating health along with gentle but persistent pressure from her children and some friends that persuaded Freda to take driving lessons. For a long time she had maintained her stubborn refusal, saying that at sixty-seven years of age, she was far too old to be learning new skills and adapting to new ideas.

However, her family, and indeed Godfrey himself, persisted and reminded her of several ladies in the village who were safely and contentedly chugging around even in their seventies and eighties. Indeed, one was over ninety and still motoring. These cheerful characters took themselves off shopping into York and Scarborough, went out for lunch and generally enjoyed a pleasant and independent lifestyle even though living in Elsinby. And so Freda, battered and advised from all sides by her family and friends, somewhat nervously rang a local driving instructor in Ashfordly and booked a series of lessons. Godfrey had said he could teach her, but she declined—she'd heard too many stories of husbands and wives falling out in such circumstances—and so she insisted on a professional instructor, adding that she did not want Godfrey in the car while she was being taught. She did not want her inexperience to bring about a heart attack in her husband!

The instructor, Brian Hatfield, was known for his skill and patience and agreed to those conditions before starting her off on the disused airfield at Stovensby. This was an ideal training ground for beginners—it was flat with wide, disused runways and no hazards, other than the occasional learner-driver. There was plenty of room and so a few learners did not create a major hazard. A few hours on the airfield taught her to use her gears, brakes and steering; it enabled her to reverse, make three-point turns and undertake emergency braking, all before going on to the public roads. She even knew about checking the oil level and water in the radiator.

It meant that when she actually ventured on to a public road for the first time at the wheel of a car, she felt confident in her own abilities—she knew she could handle a car. The lessons themselves provided Freda with a new lease of life, a new topic to discuss with family and friends while being something of a relief for her husband. In time, of course, the question of a driving test reared its menacing head. Long before the issue of a test arose, however, Freda had been persuaded to put 'L' plates on the family car, and drive around the lanes, even visiting Malton and Pickering with Godfrey as her qualified driver. He did his best neither to criticize her nor to countermand her instructor's teaching—all she needed was plenty of practical practice in driving on real roads and so, having overcome the hurdle of driving with Godfrey at her side, Freda was booked in for her first test. It was to be at Pickering at 10.15 a.m. one Thursday morning; she would drive there in Brian Hatfield's driving-school car, and she would take her test in that. On the day of her test, Godfrey said he would drive to the test centre too so that she could drive home in the family car without 'L' plates when she passed her test. That was an outward display of his confidence in her ability and there is no doubt Godfrey's very public support meant a great deal to her.

As Elsinby was part of my rural beat, I was a frequent visitor to the village and was aware of these happenings. In fact, most of the population in the village was aware of

Freda's determination to pass her driving test and everyone gave her the necessary support.

On the day of her test, for example, several sent her cards and flowers to wish her every success. Needless to say, everyone was delighted when she passed.

She drove home in the family car without 'L' plates and with Godfrey at her side, a sight not missed by the watchful eyes of those in Elsinby who were wondering how she had progressed. That evening an impromptu celebration party followed in the Hopbind Inn with Freda as the star of the moment. Her son and daughter with their own families came too and it was that kind of response that made Freda and Godfrey absolutely sure they had made the right decision by retiring to Elsinby.

Not long after Freda's success, however, Godfrey took a turn for the worse. He suffered a series of minor heart attacks, most of which incapacitated him only for brief periods, but then one afternoon he was found in his garden having suffered a massive stroke. A neighbour discovered him—Freda was not far away at the time, having afternoon tea with some friends in the village—and Dr McGee was called. Godfrey was rushed into St Aidan's Cottage hospital and immediately placed in intensive care. Sadly, the stroke paralysed him down one side of his body, robbing him of his speech and the use of his right arm and right leg. He would have to remain in hospital for an indefinite period.

It was this unwelcome development which made Freda realize she had done the right thing in learning to drive.

It had given her valuable independence and it meant she could continue her life by visiting friends, going shopping, attending to Godfrey's needs and occupying herself in and around Elsinby. I came across her from time to time and we would always find time for a chat and an exchange of news; I must say I admired her spirit and her determination to live life to the full while caring for Godfrey.

When he was in hospital, she was a familiar sight in the village, a short and rather thick-set lady with a round, warm face, spectacles and iron-grey hair; she wore a smart blue coat and carried a matching handbag when she went visiting. She would pop in to see various elderly ladies and some equally elderly gentlemen for a chat and an offer to shop for them; she would help in their gardens and generally involve herself in village matters. And she would drive off to Ashfordly, Eltering, Pickering, Malton and even York in her little family car. It all helped her cope with Godfrey's long spell of recuperation in St Aidan's.

Eventually in early November, Godfrey was considered fit to return home. Doctor McGee came to visit Freda to tell her the good news. Godfrey had recovered most of his speech along with some movement in his right leg and right arm. He could walk with the aid of a frame and was able to make his wishes known; he could even feed himself, wash his face, clean his teeth and go to the toilet, but, Dr McGee suggested, that if possible he should be given a bedroom downstairs.

With that in mind, he examined Freda's dining-room and said it would be ideal—it was close to the downstairs toilet which contained a washbasin, there was easy access to the lounge and kitchen, and there were no steps to negotiate when going outside or into the garden. All it needed was a bed, some special lighting and a few aids such as a stout handle on the wall beside the bed so that Godfrey could lever himself into a sitting position and so leave the bed for the bathroom. Doctor McGee also suggested Freda remove any rugs in case he tripped over them, then said he would wait until the necessary alterations were complete before discharging Godfrey.

For Freda, the next few days were quite frantic. There seemed to be so much to do before Godfrey's new bedroom was complete—the first thing was to buy a new single bed. Thanks to friends in the village, someone brought it home in a van and assembled it. A village electrician installed some bedside lights and another helpful character fixed the handle on the wall so that Godfrey could aid his movements in and out of bed. A host of people came and did whatever was necessary and soon Godfrey's new bedroom was ready for occupation. The day before he was due to leave hospital, Freda decided to drive into Ashfordly to buy a small television set which could be accommodated on Godfrey's chest of drawers in his new room. The shop's manager said a technician would come out first thing tomorrow morning to fit it, along with the new aerial.

And then Freda climbed into her car to drive home, by this stage feeling both tired and elated. Finally everything was ready for Godfrey to come home and she was determined to make his return as comfortable and welcoming as possible. He was expected about ten o'clock in the morning. She had even bought a bottle of champagne and a box of his favourite chocolates, a form of welcoming gift, and she would cook his favourite lunch. With all her plans buzzing around in her mind with the inevitable worry about whether she had thought of everything, Freda left Ashfordly to drive home to Elsinby. She felt sure she had done everything she could. Her journey was a distance of about six miles; she was elated, happy and smiling, singing gently to herself as she guided the family car along the quiet lanes leading home. Being November, darkness arrived early and on this occasion there was some heavy drizzle too; she had switched on her headlights, the first time she had driven in the darkness, and the wipers were coping with the persistent dampness on the outside of her windscreen. Inside, however, there was some condensation, not a lot but sufficient to slightly blur her view of the road ahead. She did not really notice that defect . . . although she did move her head closer to the screen to peer through. Within only a quarter of a mile or so, the drizzle developed into a thick fog. Her driving test and tuition had not dwelt upon the matter of driving at night or in foggy conditions—certainly not a combination of both. In spite of everything, Freda was coping with the controls and driving very carefully but visibility was poor and getting worse. Luckily, the road was quiet with little traffic from either direction.

There were no oncoming lights to dazzle her and so she stooped a little further forward to get closer to the windscreen, at the same time slowing down as she tried to keep her eyes on the verge in the thickening fog. Quite suddenly, she felt frightened—she had never had to drive in such suddenly awful conditions, but she knew she must press on. After all, it wasn't night—it wasn't even teatime yet, even if it felt like the early hours of a dreadful foggy November morning.

And then something loomed out of the fog immediately ahead. It was directly in her path. It was close, far too close . . . and before she knew what was happening, she collided with the object. There was an awful clattering noise and a shout. Not knowing what had happened, she was thrown sideways in her seat, an action in which she wrenched the steering wheel and found herself shooting across a grass verge and into a thick hawthorn hedge, now devoid of leaves. She came to rest in a gutter with the nose of the car buried in the hedge, unconscious because she had banged her head on the door pillar on the right of the windscreen. Smatterings of blood showed where the impact had occurred.

It was not known how long she remained in that condition but a passing van driver found the car in the ditch, with the elderly lady passenger still in her seat and unconscious. She was alive but he knew better than move her in case she had unseen injuries and so rang the emergency services from a roadside kiosk. I was patrolling in my van near Thackerston when the call came through.

It was not foggy on low-lying ground but, as I sped through the darkness towards the scene, I was travelling uphill on fast-rising ground and suddenly found myself enveloped with thick, dense and very wet fog. I switched on my rotating blue light because it could be seen at a greater distance than other lights in foggy conditions and did my best to reach the scene in the shortest possible time. I was first to arrive and positioned my van on the road behind the ditched car with all lights blazing, hoping and praying nothing would collide with my vehicle. In the lights of my van, I saw the car—and realized it was Freda's. And she was still slumped over the steering wheel. I made a quick examination, realized she was still alive and raced back to my van to make sure the ambulance had been called.

In Ashfordly Police Station, Alf Ventress acknowledged my call and confirmed the ambulance was *en route*. I provided a very brief situation report, and then prepared to deal with the accident. Armed with a powerful torch, I began to search the scene to see whether there were any other casualties. Sometimes, casualties were catapulted a considerable distance out of crashing vehicles and so I made a rapid but thorough search of the ground which surrounded Freda's car. And that is when I found the gents' bicycle. It was lying in front of her car, crushed between the hedge and its bonnet, and it was in a very mangled state. But there was no one with it.

With some horror, I wondered if the rider was beneath the car and so I knelt down and, with my torch, searched the entire space beneath the car, but there was no one there.

Next, I clambered over a nearby gate into the field beyond the hedge and, still in thick fog, searched for any signs of other victims, but there was none. Surely Freda hadn't collided with this bike as it lay in the ditch? The chances of that happening were far too remote—surely the bike had been on the road? Then, as so often happens, the fog suddenly lifted. One minute I was floundering around in dense foggy darkness, and the next everything was crisp and clear, if still dark. Then the ambulance arrived.

I explained the situation to the two-man crew and, after confirming that Freda was still alive if unconscious with the possibility of a head injury, we made a second search of the surroundings using powerful searchlights which were part of the ambulance's equipment. But we found no one. So where was the bike rider?

With their customary skill and efficiency, the ambulance men extracted Freda from her car, put her on to a stretcher and carried her to their vehicle. As she was being removed, though, I thought one of her arms was hanging rather limply—I feared it was broken—and the crew said they would bear that in mind. She was whisked off to Ashfordly General as I was left to measure the scene, take details of her car and take possession of any valuables she might have left in the vehicle. I radioed Alf once more to request the breakdown truck from Bernie's Garage in Aidensfield—I wanted her car removed as quickly as possible because it was a hazard—its rear end was protruding into the carriageway and its lights were not functioning. When Bernie's truck arrived, I asked him to remove the cycle too.

Alf said he would arrange for both the car and bike to be examined at Bernie's garage by vehicle experts first thing tomorrow morning—Bernie would place them in secure accommodation until we had finished with them. I wanted to know what had caused the accident. The bike's lights—front and rear—were smashed, for example, and so were those at the front of the car, but the question of inadequate lighting would arise, as would the question of whether the car had a defect, say faulty brakes, defective steering or a soft tyre. I was aware of the extremely foggy conditions which prevailed earlier, so that might also be a factor even if it was clear now. In short, I needed an account from Freda—particularly what part the bicycle had played in this accident. On the face of things, it seemed she had run into the rear of a pedal cycle in dense fog but if so, where was the rider? That was a mystery.

Having cleared the vehicles from the scene, made yet another careful but unsuccessful search for a possible cyclist casualty and taken my necessary measurements for a sketch as part of my accident report, I decided Freda's family should be told of her accident. Godfrey was in St Aidan's Cottage Hospital in Elsinby and I didn't know their son and daughter's addresses. I felt sure St Aidan's would have those details in their files and local gossip suggested Godfrey was able to communicate and comprehend.

I drove immediately to Elsinby, a matter of ten minutes from the scene of accident, and was in time to find the patients having their evening meal. Nurse Collins, one of the duty staff, spotted my arrival.

'Ah, PC Rhea! Is this a business or social call? There is plenty of tea in plenty of pots if you fancy a cup!'

'I'll accept your offer,' I was dying for a cup of lovely fresh tea after dealing with the accident. 'But first, I need to see Godfrey Holden.' And I explained my reason.

'I'll talk to Matron first,' she said. 'This is dreadful, he was really looking forward to going home in the morning. I'm not sure how this news will affect him either . . . so how is Mrs Holden? We need to tell him.'

'I don't know,' I admitted. 'I haven't been in touch with Ashfordly General just yet.'

'I'll ring them from here; they'll tell me because her husband is one of our patients,' and with no more ado she picked up a phone and called Ashfordly General, explaining the matter. I watched her nodding as she received the latest update and then she put down the phone and smiled.

'She's recovered consciousness, you'll be pleased to know.' She looked happy. 'She has had a knock on the head but her skull's not broken and it seems she has concussion. She's also got a broken arm, the right ulna, but apart from that she doesn't seem to have any injuries other than a few cuts and bruises. She'll live, Mr Rhea; she's not in any danger.'

'Did they say if her son and daughter have been informed?'

'No, they haven't, Ashfordly's not been in touch with any relatives, but they know Godfrey is here. We gave the son and daughter's addresses and home numbers. You'll need those?'

'Yes, I must make sure they're told.'

'Good, well, you go through to Rievaulx Ward; you'll see Godfrey in there and I'll bring some cups of tea through. I hope he takes this as well as he's able. Shall I sit with you both?'

'That's a great idea! Now, another question. Has a cyclist been brought in during the last hour or so? Or anyone needing emergency treatment?' and I told her the reason for my question.

'No, sorry, no one. I'd have known if anyone had been brought in, or come in voluntarily.'

'Can I ring Ashfordly to ask them? It's important I find him.'

'Be my guest.'

Ashfordly General provided the same answer. No emergency admissions had been made in the last few hours, other than Freda, and no one had walked in for treatment of the kind they might sustain in a road accident. And none of the local doctors had requested hospital treatment of their patients—but, of course, some doctor might have treated a casualty either at home or in his surgery, in which case few would know about it. I thanked Nurse Collins and Ashfordly General for their help. I then turned my attention to Godfrey.

He took the sad news remarkably well and was genuinely more concerned about Freda than his own return home. Freda's injuries would probably mean she was home fairly soon, unless complications arose and so, having broken the news to him, I obtained his son's telephone number and rang Graham from the hospital. I explained about Freda, saying I had yet to interview her about the accident but that would have to wait until her doctor gave me the necessary permission. Graham said he understood and added it had been his intention to visit his parents once his father was out of hospital—he would bring forward that visit, saying he and his wife would arrive at Howe End Cottages, Elsinby this evening. Freda and Godfrey would be in good hands—and Godfrey would return home as planned.

Next morning at 9.30 a.m. I walked down to Bernie's Garage in Aidensfield to have a look at Freda's car and the mangled bike. I wanted to record details of each before the vehicle examiners arrived. Now that I was looking at them in daylight, I could see the full extent of their damage and made notes for my accident report; the car had some moderate damage to the front, including smashed headlights and sidelights, a dented nearside wing and a broken radiator grille. Although the car had run over the bike, I could not see any damage beneath the car but testing its brakes and steering was not my job. The bike, by comparison, was a mess. A gents' blue Frejus with a 21" frame, aluminium dropped handlebars and lightweight racing wheels, it was wrecked.

The frame was twisted, the wheels buckled and the handlebars smashed. And both lights were ruined, although both contained batteries in working condition. Had the lights been showing at the time of the accident? But where was the rider? That riddle had not yet been solved.

The outcome of the vehicle examiners' tests were that Freda's car had no defects in its braking system or steering. Its wiring was up to scratch too and all lights functioned when test bulbs were fitted. Everything about the car was in very good condition—that was their verdict and they would supply me with a written report to that effect. Likewise the bike—in spite of its current condition, it was obviously a very expensive machine ordinarily kept in pristine condition, consequently it was extremely odd that no one was found with it in the aftermath of the accident. It was an enthusiast's bike, not merely one used for getting around, Frejus once being one of the favourite models in the fabulous Tour de France.

After viewing the car and the bike, I drove into Ashfordly because a thought had occurred to me—if the bike had apparently been abandoned in the aftermath of that accident, could it have been stolen? Had a thief been riding it at the time of the accident? Or was it lying unattended in the road? The owner of such an expensive machine would never allow himself to be knocked off his bike, and then leave it to God and providence while he did a runner? And why run away unless he had something to hide? I wanted to look through the stolen cycles index which was updated daily at Ashfordly Police Station because that offered one explanation.

When I arrived, I was surprised to see Inspector Harry Breckon in Ashfordly Police Station. He was the sub-divisional inspector based at Eltering, and Ashfordly was under his command, hence his periodic but infrequent visits. On the sergeant's day off, he was checking the occurrence book to ensure it was up to date and that every entry had been actioned.

'Ah, PC Rhea,' he smiled. He was a pleasant man, and popular with all his colleagues, even his subordinates. 'That accident last night—a very curious one, by all accounts, so PC Ventress tells me.'

'Yes, sir,' and I then gave him a summary of the accident with my progress to date, adding my concerns about the cycle. He nodded and expressed satisfaction with my actions so far.

When I had finished, he said, 'So, PC Rhea, are we talking about a careless driving prosecution here? It does seem as if Mrs Holden was careless—running into a cyclist from the rear. That smacks of carelessness, although I do appreciate it was very foggy at the time. But drivers should drive according to the conditions, foggy or otherwise.'

'I think the bike might have been stolen, sir, which could explain why the rider vanished from the scene. I'm here to check our reports of stolen bikes.'

'In which case he might have been riding without lights, eh? To conceal himself after committing the crime? It wasn't late, was it? Teatime or thereabouts? Not fully dark?'

'That's very possible, sir. I would also like to check surgeries and do another survey of local hospitals—if he got knocked off that bike he could be injured. If we don't find him, we'll have difficulty getting the necessary evidence for a prosecution, especially when there's doubt as to whether the bike was showing lights,' I countered. 'And it might have been lying in the road, unattended.'

'Points taken, PC Rhea. We mustn't jump to conclusions.'

'I haven't interviewed Mrs Holden yet. She's not fit to be questioned so I have no account of what really happened. I'll be checking with the hospital later today to see if she can be interviewed, after the doctor has done his rounds.'

'Good, well it seems you're doing a good job with this one. Let me have your accident report in due course—and don't forget that if there is question of careless driving, you'll have to serve Mrs Holden with a Notice of Intended Prosecution within fourteen days of the accident.'

With that parting shot, he left me to plough through the latest list of stolen cycles—hundreds of them but it included all those stolen and not recovered during the last two years. I had a feeling this crime was much more recent and fortunately the dates of the thefts were listed. And then I found it—the theft of a gents' blue racing Frejus with lightweight trim and wheels . . . it had been taken from outside a café in Eltering two days ago. But was it the bike which had been involved in Freda's accident?

I rang Eltering Police to ask that an officer contact the owner with a request that he visit Aidensfield Garage to examine the cycle. I needed a statement to confirm or deny ownership of the machine and so I would have to accompany him.

He rang me the same day and we arranged to meet at the garage; I went a few minutes early to warn Bernie to have the cycle available. When the loser arrived, he was a slender, grey-haired man called Joseph Cookson. A retired accountant, he'd had the Frejus for several years, he told me, and it was his pride and joy. He'd used it for racing as a young man and had once won the Northern Counties Road Race championship on the cycle. He was devastated when he saw the remains of his precious cycle and said it was beyond repair although he did confirm it was his property—the serial number on the frame established that. I asked if he had been riding the machine at the time of the accident, and he said, 'No.' He could prove it, he added, because he was at the dentist's, and he gave me the address so I could confirm his story. The cycle had been stolen before that visit.

I provided him with an account of the accident, but said I had not yet interviewed the car driver in question. I provided him with Freda's name and address and suggested he should contact her insurance company about compensation for his loss. He said he would do that. He asked if he could remove the cycle and take it home, but I felt it should remain at the garage until the question of prosecuting Freda had been determined.

He understood; I said I would get in touch with him once the situation was known.

Meanwhile, I instigated enquiries at hospitals and surgeries throughout Ryedale and the moors to see whether anyone had been admitted with injuries which might be consistent with involvement in a road traffic accident. Despite our efforts, we failed to trace anyone—I knew of experienced racing cyclists who could tumble from their machines and survive without injury.

It was three days later when doctors allowed me to visit Freda in St Aidan's Cottage Hospital. I suggested her son, Graham, attended too as she would need his support. For my accident report, I required personal facts such as her date of birth; I also needed to inspect her driving licence and insurance for the car, and so my visit became something of an ordeal for her. Fortunately Graham understood the official requirements and the purpose of my visit. When it came to asking her what had happened, tears appeared in her eyes and she shook her head, clutching Graham's hand for emotional support.

'Try to tell PC Rhea, Mum,' he spoke softly. 'He needs it for his report.'

'But I don't know what happened; I can't remember anything except it was very foggy and the next thing I knew was when I woke up in here.'

'But you remember driving along that road?'

'Oh yes, I'd been to Ashfordly to get some things ready for Godfrey coming home. It was growing dark so I wanted to get home and then I ran into the fog . . . it was awful, Mr Rhea, so dense and dark . . . and then I woke up in here.'

'So you know nothing of what happened?'

'No, except Graham has told me about the bicycle, but I can't remember anything about that. And how is the cyclist?'

'We haven't found him yet, that's the odd thing. The cycle was stolen from Pickering so its owner wasn't riding it at the time. But I think the rider was quite skilled—experienced cyclists can often take a fall without getting hurt, they roll into a ball and get clear of trouble . . . but what interests us is whether the bike was displaying a back light, or any lights.'

'I just don't know'—her eyes became moist—'I wish I did know but I don't.'

'The cycle owner might contact you about insurance for the bike—that is quite standard practice. If he does, just refer him to your insurance company. There is no doubt your car hit the cycle—I saw the aftermath.'

'Yes, of course. Does that mean I am responsible?'

'The driver of a car is generally responsible for what occurs while driving on a road, but in a case like this, where there is a lot of doubt about the precise circumstances, you might not be culpable. A lot hinges on whether the cycle was on the same side of the road as you and going your way, while displaying a red rear light, especially in foggy conditions.'

'I don't know,' she repeated. 'I just don't know.'

Having conducted my short interview, I did not feel I should deliver to her the Notice of Intended Prosecution. This was a legal formality in cases where drivers of motor vehicles could face prosecution for certain serious traffic offences—it was a warning which gave them time to organize their defence, and it must be delivered within fourteen days of the accident or incident in question. It could be done either verbally or in writing, and if in writing delivered either by hand, registered post or recorded delivery. I had a typed copy of the notice ready to hand to Freda, but I felt it was not appropriate at this particular moment. So I withheld any reference to it, or to a likely court appearance—a few days remained for that requirement to be fulfilled. I wanted to complete my report and then recommend no prosecution. In my view, there was insufficient evidence to proceed in court.

And that is what transpired. My completed and very detailed report highlighted the fact that the cyclist in question had stolen the bike and apparently ridden it in dark and foggy conditions without a rear light. I stressed I had not found any other drivers who were on that road at the material time and who might have also seen the cyclist. I added that Mrs Holden's car was in good condition with no defects, and there is no reason to believe she was driving carelessly or dangerously. I added that it was possible the cycle was lying in the road with no one in attendance—quite literally, having been stolen, it could have fallen off the back of a lorry.

When submitting my report, I said I had not yet served the required Notice of Intended Prosecution due to the sickness of the driver concerned, but sufficient time remained for that procedure if it was decided she would be summoned to court. Having read my report, and considered the recommendations of the sub-divisional inspector, the superintendent decided upon no further action against Freda. I was relieved and drove straight round to Godfrey's home to tell him and his family—they would break the news to her.

Later, I received a letter of thanks from Graham Holden, saying how the family appreciated my actions during what for them was a harrowing time but in my view I had done nothing more than my duty. Nonetheless, I think my old training sergeant would have approved. The villain of the piece was the thief whose greedy actions so devastatingly affected the lives of several people—Freda said she would never drive again but she now had the task of making a full recovery so she could care for Godfrey.

And in force headquarters, a clerk would place a sticker on a map to record a minor accident involving a car and a pedal cycle on a country road near Aidensfield.

CHAPTER SIX

One area of duty in which the police can impress the public with their knowledge and skill is within the world of crime prevention. This is considered one of the prime duties of a police officer—indeed, the earliest definition of a constable, which dates to the foundation of the modern police service, said that his or her duties include the preservation of the peace, the prevention and detection of crime, the protection of life and property and the maintenance of public order. Taken as a whole, this provides a wide-ranging responsibility which, due to the nature of police work, can never be subjected to a precise interpretation. Within each of those duties lies many facets which means that police officers must exercise discretion when enforcing the law, providing advice or going about their daily work; without that discretion we could produce a police state.

Because crime prevention is such an important element of police work, it entails more than just standing on a street corner in police uniform, although that alone does prevent a considerable number of minor offences. The sight of a police uniform makes people behave and that is no bad thing. However, active crime prevention (rather than the passive)—and most police forces have full-time crime prevention officers—involves a whole range of skills, chiefly of an advisory nature some of which require the police to be ahead of criminals in their thinking. Anticipating the next popular form of crime is not an exact science, but police officers can often notice the beginnings of a new trend.

In simple terms, therefore, crime prevention means advising the public how to halt, prevent or frustrate criminals like thieves, burglars, confidence tricksters, financial crooks, identity stealers and other rogues.

Sceptics might argue that genuine crime prevention is nothing more than common sense. In very basic terms that is true—if you don't want something stealing, you lock it away or keep it out of sight. You don't put temptation in the way of a thief. You lock the doors and windows of your house, shop, caravan or car if you leave them unattended, you secure your bicycle and never leave valuables lying around. You don't open a handbag or wallet full of money in a public place. You don't let people into your home unless you know who they are and you don't buy goods at the door unless you have ordered them in advance. It's basic common sense, isn't it?

These are very simple, straightforward precautions for everyday situations, but in addition to crimes that come to the notice of the police, there is a huge amount which is not recorded. That makes official crime statistics quite useless with annual fluctuations and detection figures being equally meaningless. So how do the police know that unknown crimes are not reported? It is easy—how many businesses or councils never report the theft of things like pens, envelopes, paper clips, minor spare parts for cars, pieces of meat, baked buns or other manufactured products? These are crimes—staff who remove them without authority are stealing.

How many hotels never report the loss of towels, bars of soap and even irons and framed pictures from bedrooms? I knew one hotel which had a trouser press stolen from a bedroom, but that *was* reported. Hotel theft is also an area of crime that is seldom, if ever, reported to the police and it does not therefore feature in the official figures. The exception would be if someone managed to get into a guest's bedroom to steal the guest's belongings. That sort of crime is reported because the guest is the victim—it seems that if the guest is the culprit, then no such report is made.

In a similar vein, how many ladies leave their handbags in vulnerable places, if only momentarily, and then find them, or some of their contents, missing? Even today, I see women pushing trolleys around supermarkets with their handbags on display, many open in readiness for the cash point, making a tempting offer to a quick-thinking thief. More than likely, stolen handbags or contents will be recorded as lost property rather than a crime—it's one way of keeping the crime figures low!

Some years ago, I was discussing shoplifting with the owner of a large store and he told me he was quite happy that the current level of theft from his shop should continue. 'I expect to lose about 2 per cent of my stock every year to shoplifters,' he said. 'It shows that our marketing is working, we are making our goods appealing.' In the famous words of those wonderful comedians, Eric Morecambe and Ernie Wise, 'There's no answer to that.'

Not surprisingly, in my work as the village constable of Aidensfield, I was expected to offer crime prevention advice as part of my normal duties.

Inevitably, this was done in conjunction with other work—for example, if I walked into someone's cottage and noticed the kitchen window had a broken fastener, I would advise the householder to get it repaired. Simple common sense, it might be said, but it is surprising how many householders never notice such defects in their own premises. It was also surprising how many left windows open when they were absent—even open bedroom windows can provide entry points for a determined burglar.

Another piece of advice was never to leave door keys in the locks—remove them and keep them in a safe place. An opportunist thief can swiftly place his hand inside the door and remove the key—then he can enter the house at any suitable moment. This also applies to shops and offices—I advised several shopkeepers not to leave the shop keys in the front door lock. After all, it does take some time to replace locks or obtain replacement keys, and that provides an ample opportunity for a thief.

Leaving a light in the house when one is out during the hours of darkness is also very sensible—but not the front hall light! People don't live in front halls, they live in kitchens or lounges or even bedrooms, so a house in darkness, except for the front hall light, is an immediate announcement of the occupier's absence. The idea of leaving a light burning is to make the house seem occupied. And close all the ground-floor curtains at night so prevent snoopers peering in to see what valuables you might own.

Leaving cars keys in the ignition is another way making an offering to a thief, even if the car is parked on your own drive or you have left it only momentarily to pay for a tank of petrol or to post a letter. Recently, a man did just that—he left the keys in his car while he popped into a motorway service station to pay for petrol and when he emerged, his car had gone.

My part of England is a very busy and popular tourist area and it is disheartening at times to learn how many visitors leave valuables on show in their cars when they park at beauty spots to go for a short walk. One woman left her car for only ten minutes in a busy tourist area to give her dog a quick walk, but her handbag, camera and binoculars were left on show. She had locked her car doors and windows, but when she returned, they had all been stolen—the thief had smashed a window, opened a door and removed everything. And her handbag contained all her holiday money, more than £80 in cash.

To provide good workable advice for every likely situation is practically impossible and so most police officers will act spontaneously whenever a situation arises—and that can have more impact than a staged show of crime prevention techniques and lectures. Nonetheless, most police forces despatch their crime prevention teams to mount exhibitions at places where members of the public gather in large numbers, such as supermarkets and major departmental stores, agricultural shows, pop concerts, top sporting fixtures, open days at country houses and similar functions.

I am sure some good comes from such efforts. Not far from my patch at Aidensfield, however, it seemed someone was sneaking around, unseen and unheard by villagers, and creating some alarm through his (or perhaps her) highly unconventional crime prevention technique.

It is difficult to know for how long and how often the mystery caller had been at work, but my first indication that something peculiar was afoot occurred one November morning. I received a phone call from a resident of Briggsby, one of the smaller villages on my patch. It was little more than a hamlet with no pub and the only shop, which doubled as a post office, was in the front room of Mrs Bonney Brown's cottage. The village, which lay just off the main road into Ashfordly, comprised a short street with rows of pretty stone cottages at each side, and a few farms around the outskirts. It was only a mile from Ashfordly by road which meant many of the residents would walk into town, especially on market day—and the walk was shorter and quicker if one went across the fields. Unfortunately, there was no established footpath across the fields which meant it was a very muddy experience for most of the year.

However, shortly after nine one Monday morning I was working in my Aidensfield office. As usual for a day shift, I was busy completing files to take to Ashfordly Police Station for the sergeant's signature and onward early transmission to Divisional HQ when I picked up the phone which was shrilling.

'PC Rhea, Aidensfield.'

'Now then,' said a strong masculine voice with a North Yorkshire accent. 'I think you'd better come and see me, Mr Rhea, summat funny's going on.'

'Funny?'

'Aye, very funny.'

'Like what?'

'Like I've never known it before, that's what. Can you come and see me?'

'Is it urgent?'

'Now you tell me, Mr Rhea, you're used to this sort of carry on and I'm not. I don't know whether to think it's urgent or not. I'd say it wasn't a matter of life and death, if that's what you mean.'

'So what's happened?'

'Happened? You tell me! By gum, there's some queer goings-on nowadays, Mr Rhea. So you'll come and see me?'

'I will, and then you might explain. Say in half an hour?'

'Aye, half an hour'll be fine, it means I can fettle my pigs. I'll get the missus to put t' kettle on and she's got some smashing apple pie she made yesterday and mebbe a bit of custard and some ginger bread to go with it.'

'I've just had my breakfast,' I said.

'That's no excuse, young lads like you have to keep well fed, so you'll be here in half an hour?'

'I will, but first, who's calling and where do you live?'

'Oh, well, it's me. We had a chat last Friday in Ashfordly market, I was telling you about them pigs of mine . . .'

'Oh, right, I remember. So where do you live?'

'Briggsby. I thought you knew that.'

'Right, of course,' I was struggling to remember the conversation in question. 'Is it Harry Irvine?'

'Nay, don't be so daft, lad, it's me. Joe Ridley.'

'Oh, of course, Joe. I didn't recognize your voice.'

'Not many folks do, but it doesn't alter t'fact it's still me. Anyroad, half an hour.' And his phone went dead. He still hadn't told me where he lived but in a place like Briggsby, I would quickly locate him. I checked with my copy of the Electoral Register and discovered he and his wife, May, lived at Ash Tree House, an extensive smallholding at the bottom of the village. Now I could envisage him. Some time earlier, I'd been to sign a pig movement licence.

With my paperwork complete, I declined Mary's offer of a cup of coffee before I departed, knowing I was to be treated to a massive feast in the very near future. I would pop into Ashfordly Police Station after calling on Joe Ridley—so what on earth had happened to him?

It took only a few minutes to motor to Briggsby and I drew into the yard in front of Ash Tree House, parked and went round to the back which was the practice hereabouts. Like many larger farms, the house had a pond and was surrounded by an array of stone outbuildings and wooden sheds.

Few, if any, folk went to the front door of a house when visiting on the moors; they always went to the back and here the back door was standing open.

'Hello,' I shouted as I stepped inside.

'It's open,' called a woman's voice. 'Come in.'

The door led into a dark entrance hall with a rack fall of wellington boots, overcoats, walking sticks and dog leads. The kitchen was beyond—I could see into it where a large lady wearing a butcher's apron was wrestling with a mountain of dough. She would be almost as tall as me and twice as wide with iron-grey hair held in place with slides and ribbons; her large face was rather florid but it was hot in the kitchen with a huge fire blazing and a fireside oven warm enough to take her new bread.

'Mrs Ridley?'

'Come in, Mr Rhea, our Joe won't be a minute, he's just gone down to see to his pigs. Sit yourself down, the tea's on the table and that apple pie's for you. Joe said you liked apple pie and there's a bit of gingerbread and some custard . . . best tackle that while you're waiting, eh?'

'Oh, er, right, thank you.'

A fork and spoon were laid out ready for me and so I pulled the dish of apple pie towards me, poured on the custard and began to tuck in. To be honest, it was wonderful even though I'd already demolished a hearty breakfast. As I sat in the kitchen, with May Ridley pummelling the life out of a huge pile of dough, I decided to try and discover why I was here.

'Any idea why Joe wants to see me?' I asked between mouthfuls.

'He'd best explain himself,' was her guarded response. 'It's upset him, Mr Rhea, things like that do, don't they? Upset people.'

'Well, yes, I suppose so. It's often a good idea to talk it over with other people.' I thought my response was sufficiently bland to cover anything untoward they might have experienced.

'That's just what he said, Mr Rhea. Best not to keep these things to yourself, open up and talk about it. He's not very forthcoming, though, as a rule. Bottles things up, keeps things to himself, plays his cards close to his chest, as they say.'

'I would imagine he's a bit like that.'

'More than a bit, Mr Rhea, never uses two words where one will do. Anyroad, he was a bit concerned when he found it and didn't know what to do so I said ring you, you're the local constable so you'd know what to do about it.'

'Ah, I see. So when did he find it?' I was still floundering in the dark, not knowing what had upset Joe so much—whatever it was, it had been enough to make him call in the police.

'This morning, when he came downstairs. He said nowt about it for ages, got his breakfast, went out to do up as he allus does, fed the pigs and cats and dogs and hens and geese and ducks, then came in for his second breakfast . . .'

'Second breakfast?'

'He allus has two breakfasts, Mr Rhea, his first one on getting up before going out, and his second one after coming in from when he goes out. Then after it he goes out again until 'lowance time when he comes in for a sandwich and mebbe a mug o' tea, and then he'll go out again till half twelve, then he comes in for his dinner. Half twelve on the dot, he's a man of habit, Mr Rhea.'

'It's obviously a busy life, Mrs Ridley.'

'It is that, Mr Rhea, so you can see why he doesn't like things to upset him, gets his routine all mixed up and then *he's* mixed up all day, never gets caught up with himself . . . so he'll be in soon for his second breakfast, I've got it warming. He's a bit confused today with all that's happened, he's got behind with his jobs.'

Try as I might, without asking another direct question, I failed to elicit from May the precise cause of Joe's unhappiness and so we chatted about the weather, the state of farming today, the price of pigs and eggs and the usual topics in rural life. And then Joe came in. He hung his hat on the stand in the hall and, without a word to anyone, went across to the kitchen sink, washed his hands, dried them and then went to the table. As he was sitting down, May, as if by magic, produced from the side oven a huge plate of breakfast—bacon, sausages, eggs and mushrooms—and set it before him. Still without uttering a word, he began to eat it without looking to left and right, and so I continued with my slice of apple pie. As I was nearing its end, a second slice appeared from May, with more custard, and so Joe and I kept each other silent munching company. We finished almost together.

He wiped his mouth with a handkerchief, belched and said, 'So, Mr Rhea, what do you make of it?'

'It's very nice pie,' I smiled. 'Lovely.'

'No, I meant this carry on.'

'I'm not sure what's happened,' I admitted. 'I know you've had some kind of nasty experience . . .'

'Oh, didn't I tell you?'

'No,' I said briefly.

'Right, well, it was this,' and he left his chair and went over to the mantelpiece to produce a piece of paper tucked behind a candlestick. He brought it to the table, sat down and handed it to me. It was a torn piece of lined paper, the sort one might find in a child's exercise book or even a writing pad, and it bore a brief message in pencil. In capital letters which did not seem the work of someone very fluent with a pen or pencil, it said, I COULD HAVE PINCHED EVERYTHING YOU'VE GOT. There was nothing else on the paper.

I turned it over and it was blank on the reverse. 'So where did this come from?'

'You tell me,' he said. 'Just you tell me, Mr Rhea.'

'You didn't write it? Or your wife?'

'Nay, lad, we did not. It was here, on this table this morning when I came downstairs. Lying in t'middle with a salt pot on top to anchor it down. And it wasn't there when we went up to bed last night.'

'So how did it get here?'

'That's what I want to know, Mr Rhea. That's why I called you in. Somebody put it there overnight. Not us, Mr Rhea, and we've nobody staying here, so who else could it be, eh? Just you tell me that.'

'Are you saying somebody has entered your house at night while you were both in bed, and left this note?'

'That's just what I am saying, Mr Rhea. Exactly.'

'So how did they get in?'

'Through t'scullery window. Here, I'll show you.'

He left the table and I followed him into the scullery, a small, cold room at the back of the house. It was equipped with a washbasin, a draining board, racks on the wall for crockery and little else. Then I saw the muddy footprint on the draining board below the window.

'I left that for you to see,' he said. 'Whoever it was slid that window back, climbed in, left his print on that draining board and put this note on the table.'

'Hmm. So has anything been stolen?'

'Nowt, Mr Rhea. That's the funny thing about all this . . . he breaks into my house in the dead of night and does nowt except leave a note saying he could have pinched everything I own.'

'But you're sure he took nothing?'

'I am. Now what sort of a chap does that, Mr Rhea. You tell me.'

'A very strange sort of a chap!' I said. 'So are you both sure nothing's been taken? Money? Ornaments? Silverware? Jewellery? Something belonging to Mrs Ridley?'

'Like I said, absolutely nowt, Mr Rhea, and we've none of that finery you mention, not in this house, and so far as money's concerned, I've got all my cash hidden about the place; he'd never find it, never in a month of Sundays. I've checked it and it's all there, down to t' last ha'penny.'

'Well, it's not often people break into houses at night to leave things behind, or to offer advice, but this looks as if you've had such a visitor. He seems to be advising you to lock up at night but it's a queer way of doing so.'

'Lock up? We never lock up at night, Mr Rhea, never have done and never will. There's no need, is there? Besides, I like the windows open, upstairs and down, so fresh air's allus circulating in the house and I can hear my pigs if summat goes wrong.'

'You never heard them last night? Your dogs barking, or the geese sounding off?' Geese are wonderful guardians, honking loudly at the slightest noise or activity.

'Not a sound, Mr Rhea.'

'So what time did you come downstairs this morning?'

'The usual time, Mr Rhea.'

'And when is that?'

'Half five, Mr Rhea! I can't abide lying in bed until half the day's gone, not when I've things to do.'

'And what time did you go to bed?'

'It was latish, I had some bookwork to get done. Nine o'clock, mebbe as late as half past.'

'Both of you?'

'Aye.'

There was a pause as I tried to determine my next move. I wasn't quite sure what to do about this, but it was clear that Joe expected some kind of professional response from me. He sat and waited, looking at me almost with the unblinking eyes of a young pup as I struggled to think of something sensible.

'This is a bit of puzzle, Mr Ridley,' I said.

'Aye, I know.'

'I mean, it's a legal puzzle as well,' I said. 'So far as I know, no crime has been committed—nothing's been stolen or damaged; you and your wife were not attacked; he's not tried to set fire to the house . . .'

'There must be summat, Mr Rhea! Folks must be allowed to sleep peacefully in their beds at night. You can't have folks coming into your house while you're asleep, just like that, without being asked and without as much as a by-your-leave.'

'There is a trespass, yes, which does mean it is unlawful but it is not a matter for the police. Trespass is a civil offence, not a criminal one. Now, if he had come into the house, either through an open window or door, or if he'd broken in with the intention of stealing, raping, causing malicious damage or setting fire to your house, then he would have committed burglary or housebreaking, depending on the time of his entry. Even if he did nothing, he would still be guilty if any of those crimes was his intention when he entered. But if his entire intention was to leave nothing more than a helpful warning note, then the police can't prosecute.'

'Well, that's a rum 'un.'

'It is odd, I agree. So what I'll do, Mr Ridley, is to take this note away with me and I will ask all my colleagues if they've come across this before. I can't think why your house has been targeted—it does seem very odd, especially being right out here in the countryside, but it might be that other folks have had similar visitations and not told us.'

'You can check the handwriting?'

'If we get other notes, we can check whether they are written by the same person, yes. With only this to go on, we can't identify who wrote these words and the paper is the sort you can buy in any stationery shop or find in any school or office. I'm wondering if we have some kind of strange character who sees himself as a do-gooder, warning people to lock their doors and windows at night. But even so, it's odd that he's found your house.'

'It's a daft way of doing it,' he said. 'Very upsetting to us folks who live here.'

'It is—one of these days, somebody's sure to catch him in the act and they might think he's a burglar—'

'And shoot him?'

'I hope it doesn't come to that, Mr Ridley! Detain him, yes, using reasonable force, but shooting's not the answer, unless he's going to shoot you. And that doesn't seem to be this chap's intention.'

After further explaining to the couple the intricacies of criminal law as it affected their particular case, I prepared to leave. I thanked them for their hospitality and assured them they had done the right thing in reporting this to me. I asked them both to keep their ears and eyes open in case they came across any other instances or gossip about it, and then asked them to inform me. Even if the intentions were noble, it was a very strange example of crime prevention, but it did persuade Mr and Mrs Ridley to lock all their downstairs doors and windows, even if it meant a forced change in a lifetime's practice. Bearing away the puzzling piece of paper I assured them I would try to find out whether any similar incidents had been reported. As I drove away, I wasn't sure whether they were satisfied with my action which, in my opinion, did seem rather negligible and uncaring even though I had explained the legal restrictions at some length. Next, I motored down to Ashfordly to report the matter and deposit some of my routine reports and files.

Fortunately, Alf Ventress was on office duty when I arrived. If anyone would know whether such a case had occurred previously it would be Alf. He listened as I explained and then smiled.

'We've had a few of these cases reported, Nick. Very odd, I must admit. Because no crimes were committed, we couldn't take any action and they weren't recorded in our files, although Eltering CID made a few enquiries, just to make sure there was nothing more sinister going on.'

'Over what sort of period, Alf? Is this something new?'

'Not really, no. It's been going on for a few years, four or five, I reckon. Quite disturbing really; some folks have got upset about it.'

'In Ashfordly and district?'

'Most of them were further afield but there were some cases near us. They were over a very wide area by all accounts. No harm done, though, and no one's been injured even if they are alarmed. He never breaks in. He always uses an open window or door. It seems folks have always locked up their properties afterwards!'

'Any idea who might be the culprit?'

'Not a clue, Nick. You could have words with Detective Sergeant Howard Bedford at Eltering, he's spent a lot of time trying to get to the bottom of it, just out of curiosity, but he's got nowhere. He thinks a lot of similar cases could have gone unreported because they are not crimes—if anyone told one of our officers, they'd not make a record of the incident so no one really knows how prevalent this is, or has been.'

'A one-man—or one-woman—crime prevention campaign?'

'Something like that, Nick. Anyway, give Howard a ring, he'll be in his office now. He knows more about it than me.'

When I spoke to the detective sergeant and provided a detailed account of the Briggsby case, he was very interested and said it had many similarities with others that had come to his notice.

'There is a sort of pattern, Nick,' he said. 'Not so much in the locations where it happens, but because all the cases I've heard about were in farms or smallholdings. I've not been told of any in suburban houses or town houses, not even houses or cottages in villages—they've all been out in the countryside. I suppose people living in packed communities take more care about locking up their homes while country folk tend not to bother—if so, why is he targeting farms, and how does he select his targets? In other words, what's he—or she—doing on those premises in the middle of the night? I'd be grateful for any help you can give. I'm keeping a note of the ones I learn about and have them all plotted on a map in my office even though they're not really any concern of the police. I'm just curious about them!'

'Do they happen at any particular time of year?' I asked.

'Well, yes, when the nights are closing in. Late autumn and winter as a rule. That's often our busiest time for sneak thieves, burglars and the like, as you know. It's when I'd expect a spate of crimes that happen under cover of darkness—but not somebody going round giving advice like this!'

We chatted for a while about some of the individual cases that had come to his notice, but the identity of the culprit was completely unknown to him.

'As you are aware, Nick, when we get a running series of crimes—car theft, burglaries or whatever—we often know, or have some very strong ideas, about who's done it. It's usually just a case of proving it or catching the rogues red-handed. But in this case, I haven't a clue. I've asked around other divisions, by the way, and it's not happening there—it seems to be confined to our part of the North Riding.'

I promised to let him know of any other instances which might occur on the Aidensfield beat and he said he would reciprocate—I think he was pleased to find another police officer who wanted to delve into this peculiar activity, if only for his own satisfaction. When I left Ashfordly Police Station I returned to the Ridleys' smallholding but Joe was out somewhere seeing to his livestock. I told May what had transpired and she said she would tell her husband.

And there, I thought, the matter had come to an end. It wasn't a very satisfactory conclusion but it was all we could do in the circumstances. A shadowy crime prevention adviser on the loose . . . a ghostly do-gooder and perhaps someone who had, in all honesty, prevented a few crimes. I wondered if his specialized methods were more effective than those officially adopted by the police?

The phantom note-leaver of Briggsby provided much intrigue within police circles even if he was not a criminal. I felt sure he regarded himself as a do-gooder, even if his methods were highly original, more than a little peculiar and even frightening. In that sense, he was akin to many priests, vicars and ministers of religion because their lives were spent trying to do good to others, and to persuade others to do good amongst themselves and towards the rest of humanity.

It might be for that basic reason that churches, chapels and other places of divine worship were constantly at risk from thieves if only because their doors were open for most of the day. The added factor, of course, was that many were packed with rich pickings for thieves—church ornaments and furnishing were valuable, while a lot of them left money lying around in open plates or in portable collecting boxes. The theory was that only the very worst and most evil of the dregs of society would attack and rob a church. And so they did.

Some priests, vicars and ministers did not wish to prosecute thieves. As one said to me, 'Surely, PC Rhea, our duty is to help the poor? So if a poor person came to my church to ask for help, I would give it either in cash or in kind. So why can't a poor person help himself to a few pounds from our collection plate if it is readily available? His need might be more urgent and greater than mine or the church's, and if I am not around to donate the money to him, I see nothing wrong in him helping himself.'

It was not easy to argue against that logic and it might explain why so many places of divine worship, as the law defined them, were left open with cash on display in a collecting plate. Picking up money from such a place is perhaps not as bad as breaking open an offertory box to steal the contents, or removing valuables and other antiques from within the church.

Our criminal law has always dealt severely with those who steal from 'places of divine worship' and until 1968, the crime was known as sacrilege. It was specified in the Larceny Act of 1916, section 24. It was committed by anyone breaking and entering a place of divine worship and committing a felony therein. It was also committed by anyone who broke out of a place of divine worship, having committed a felony therein. Felonies were serious crimes such as murder, rape, robbery, theft or arson and the term 'breaking' included opening a closed but unlocked door.

It meant that merely walking into a church through an open door and stealing something was not sacrilege—there was no 'breaking.' That would be regarded as simple larceny, otherwise known as theft. Likewise, breaking into a church with the *intention* of committing a felony was not sacrilege either—to constitute the crime, the felony had to be committed. In such a case, the crime would be recorded as housebreaking, a church being the house of God. Exactly what constituted a place of divine worship was open to interpretation—for example, was a small wooden shed used by some obscure religious sect a place of divine worship? Often, it was a matter for a court to decide.

The crime of sacrilege was abolished by the Theft Act of 1968 when all 'breaking and entering' offences were reclassified as burglary and so legal arguments about what constituted a place of divine worship could be ignored.

In spite of all these legal aspects, one of my constant duties was to remind priests, vicars and ministers of the need to take as many steps as possible to prevent crimes within their churches and chapels. Not all of them agreed, for reasons I have already highlighted, but I always made a point of regularly visiting all the churches and chapels within my beat, if only to show a uniformed presence once in a while. There were a lot of churches and chapels on my patch—many were Roman Catholic due to the presence of Maddleskirk Abbey and its complement of monks who served small village churches from the abbey. Most of the villages also had an Anglican church and some had Methodist chapels. Faiths like Jehovah's Witnesses, the Quakers and even the Russian Orthodox church were also represented. Such places were a magnet for tourists and visitors but they were also a magnet for thieves who would steal altar cloths, kneelers, candlesticks, antique chairs and desks, pictures, silverware, like chalices, and any valuable object or cash they could find.

The sight of a uniformed bobby on patrol was always a good deterrent and, where necessary, I would pay a visit to the parish priest or incumbent if I thought some positive crime prevention measures were necessary.

Some advice was very simple, such as emptying the collection plate every day—visitors would always drop a few coins into a plate if it was left at the back of the church. During my time at Aidensfield, the theft of offertory boxes was prevalent because they were often portable and made of wood—and so the advice, expensive though it could be, was to fashion them from metal, lock them and lodge them in a secure place, such as a hole in the wall. Even so, some villains broke down those walls! It might be argued that a sensible alternative was to always leave a few shillings on open display in a collection plate at the back of the church, the theory being that an opportunist thief would take that instead of breaking open a more secure collection box. And most men of religion don't mind such moneys going to deserving causes!

Substituting valuable altar furnishings, especially silverware and candlesticks, with replicas was another suggestion, and yet a further one, which has developed in more recent times, is to fashion a reinforced glass screen either at the back of the church or in front of the altar with a secure door to prevent unauthorized access to the rest of the premises. Thus visitors can see the interior while being kept at a safe distance. Happily, many parish churches and chapels have skilled members of their congregations who will carry out those kind of major alterations and security measures at a minimum cost but the penalty of leaving our churches and chapels open to all is eternal vigilance and strong security measures. That is a great shame and a sad reflection on our society.

In paying close attention to the places of divine worship on my beat, I had never visited one of the most remote and probably one of the smallest churches in the moors. For one thing, it was not actually on my beat but not far from it, and secondly, I had never taken an opportunity to pay a visit while off duty. It was so deep in the moors, and so far off the beaten track that one did not merely pass by—it meant a special expedition to reach it. There always seemed to be some other thing to occupy my rather sparse spare time—like the family, especially as children aren't particularly keen on visiting remote and ancient churches.

The tiny church, dedicated to St Peter, stood in a remote moorland valley between Gelderslack and Grandstone; it was not part of any village or modern community, but lay beside Gelderslack Beck along almost a mile of green track. It had once been a chapel to a long-vanished abbey and was a former Roman Catholic church dating to Saxon times, with some Norman additions. It had been taken over by the Anglicans late in the sixteenth century during the Reformation, but over the years had gradually fallen into disuse. Now, it was little more than a shell but not quite derelict—indeed, it was occasionally used for services and I recall a wedding being celebrated there. It was served by the vicar of Grandstone who allowed the Catholics to return from time to time on special occasions, like the Feast of St Peter and St Paul. And one of its unique features was that it was never locked, day or night.

Coincidentally, our method of patrolling was changing around that time. This was due to motor vehicles being allocated to village bobbies—it meant we could patrol larger areas within the eight-hour period of our shifts and so we found ourselves covering neighbouring beats. In theory it meant we were not on call for twenty-four hours per day because someone else was always out there on patrol—but it didn't stop people knocking on our doors at odd times! The public had no idea when we were on duty or off—the fact remained that a country bobby was expected, by the people, to be always on duty.

And so it was I found myself patrolling Slemmington rural beat in addition to my own. The resident constable, PC Jim Collins, was having a few days' holiday and I looked forward to seeing a different part of the moors and to meeting different people. On the morning I was due to patrol his patch, I collected my local *Gazette and Herald* and found it contained a story about St Peter's lonely little church—apparently a colony of Daubenton's bats had taken up residence in the nave where they had established a nursery roost and the problem was what to do about them.

In the 1960s, bats, like other wild animals, enjoyed no particular protection—the Wildlife and Countryside Act of 1981 provided the strong protection now available. Because bats of various species tend to make a mess and produce a nasty smell while roosting or inhabiting a building, the church authorities decided to try and persuade them to leave, one suggestion being the incorporation of a stuffed owl within the church.

Due to the fuss, I thought I would have a look at the church during my patrol. It was a wonderful drive across the heights of the moors, and I could justify my visit by claiming I was on a crime prevention mission. After all, any church that remains open for twenty-four hours per day should surely need some kind of protection—even from bats. Through my visit, I might be able to make recommendations—but not for the bats.

Dropping steeply into the valley of Gelderslack Beck, I arrived at the end of the rough lane that led to the little building, parked and decided to walk the rest of the way. It took about fifteen minutes. When I arrived, I found the door standing open and soon realized there was a visitor inside. I saw him—a man in his early fifties with a woolly hat, waterproof jacket and rucksack. He noticed my arrival and smiled.

'Good morning,' he was well spoken with a local accent. 'It's not often we see the constabulary here!'

'I am patrolling the area today,' I told him. 'I thought I would come and see the famous bats!'

'They're up there,' He pointed into a corner of the rafters, very close to the joists of the bell-tower at the back of the small nave. 'Not many, twenty or thirty, I'd say.'

'Daubenton's it said in the paper,' I tried to sound knowledgeable. 'Are they rare?'

'Not really, but apart when they're breeding, like these are now, they tend to be solitary. They like swooping over water to catch flies, so they tend to live near rivers, ponds and lakes. Even though they are blind, they can skim the surface to catch mayflies and so on at night.'

'We've pipistrelles around our house at Aidensfield,' I said. 'We see lots of those.'

He then gave me a brief lecture on Daubenton's bats—a pair only produces one youngster per year for example—and then looked at his watch and said he must be getting on. He was meeting someone in Eltering. As he strode away, I spent a few minutes looking at the bats, and then toured the little church, admiring its ancient walls, font, pulpit and general design. Then, as I tend to do in churches, I went to the back to see if there was a collection box of any kind because I liked to make a contribution to maintain the fabric—and there was a dish on the rear window ledge. It was low enough for anyone to see and when I produced a half-crown to drop it in, I noticed a piece of paper resting on top of a few more coins. It was lined paper, the sort that might come from an exercise book and when I looked at it, there was a note in capital letters, written in pencil. It said, I COULD HAVE STOLEN ALL THIS MONEY. YOU SHOULD TAKE MORE CARE OF IT. And there was no signature.

That man! I dashed to the doorway but there was no sign of him and I had no idea whether he'd used the main path to leave the church, or whether he had taken a minor route through the surrounding wood.

As I hurried away, hoping to catch up with him, I realized he could be our phantom note-dropper. And I recognized a reason for him visiting remote farms in the hours of darkness—bats! That could explain why he had appeared on lonely farmsteads in the dead of night and noticed a possible opportunity for a thief. . . .

When I returned to my van, there was no sign of him and so, on my way home later that day, I called again at the Ridleys' smallholding in Briggsby. Joe was in the house, having a cup of tea and huge slice of fruit cake. He asked me to join him and, as I munched, I told him what had happened earlier that day, and then mentioned bats.

'Oh aye,' he nodded vigorously. 'We've bats in one of our outbuildings. We get all sort o' folks coming to look at 'em—I told 'em they can come whenever they like—but don't ask me if them bats are special. I know nowt about bats except they keep flies down and they're no trouble in my outbuildings. Better in there than in this house, eh?' and he chuckled.

He seemed to agree that one of the bat enthusiasts could have left the note—and they did have his permission to visit the site at any time—and I think I had convinced him I had done something positive about his strange visitor. And he assured me he now locked his doors and windows each night—but only on the ground floor.

Before returning home to book off duty, I called at Ashfordly Police Station to acquaint Alf Ventress with my news and then rang Detective Sergeant Bedford at Eltering. He listened with evident interest and thought I could be right—when he could find the time, he would visit all the other reported sites of mysterious notes to see if those places had bats in their buildings. A few weeks later, he rang me at home to say he had made those visits and, yes, all had bats on the premises. It seemed as if my theory might have some substance.

But we never found that man although we received no more reports of mysterious crime prevention advisers.

CHAPTER SEVEN

Travelling around my beat on the small but official 198cc two-stroke Francis Barnett motorcycle was a sure way of always being on view to my 'parishioners'. Although they might not see me, they could always hear me because the sound of the engine was highly distinctive, even over a considerable distance. Villains and poachers could hear me long before I arrived and so terminate or abandon their intended acts of evil—in that case, the presence of the bike was a form of crime prevention!

By comparison, the grey Mini-van that replaced the bike was not so prominent—it looked and sounded just like any other Mini-van, its only distinction being the word POLICE along each side and the blue rotating light on the roof. It was quieter than the motorbike too and the sound of its approach was just like any other small vehicle.

Although I spent a good deal of my time merely driving around 'to show the flag' as one old sergeant put it, I did spend considerable periods away from main roads and therefore beyond the sight of the general public. Among such occasions were my visits to rather remote moorland farms and huge country houses, many of which stood a mile or more from a public road. Indeed, one splendid house was at least two miles along a narrow, hilly and winding route which could be fiendish in wintertime. Quite often, on such visits, my approach was announced by the sound of my motorbike chugging along the drive or later the sight of the little grey van with its helmet-shaped blue lamp on top.

The very nature of those approach roads was such that people in the distant house or grounds were aware of approaching visitors long before they arrived, either on foot or by vehicle. In some ways, it was like a siege mentality, rather in the manner of our ancestors who built castles on hilltops so they could keep watch for an approaching enemy. To be forewarned is to be forearmed.

When I was in what might be termed my 'crime prevention mode' I was often of the opinion that a surprise visit or nefarious approach to such premises was almost impossible, even under cover of darkness. It showed that the builders of such houses and farms were very shrewd in their advance planning and, if one was honest, their caution was always justified. Without doubt a long approach provided a degree of privacy and valuable protection to remote homes, farms and businesses, especially if there was a dog along the route which barked at strangers, or a flock of geese which gabbled a warning.

My visits to farms and large country houses were generally for two basic reasons. The first was when the farm or big house kept or traded in livestock such as cattle, pigs and sheep because I had to check their stock registers and movement records at least once every three months. This was one of the measures used to prevent the spread of contagious diseases of animals. The second routine reason was to renew any firearm certificates or shotgun certificates held by the householders.

Such renewals came around every three years, although if new firearms were purchased or old ones dispensed with, then the relevant certificates had to be amended. Those records were administered by the police, hence my involvement.

Occasionally, there were other reasons for visiting such premises, one being to warn the householders when specialist criminals were known to be at work in the locality, or even if they were anticipated. From time to time, we would receive information from neighbouring police forces if specialist villains were known to be operating in their areas. Being a rural county, we had a lot in common with Cumberland, Westmorland, the East Riding, West Riding and County Durham. Those kind of villains might include antique thieves or lead strippers who raided country houses, or livestock thieves who stole sheep, cattle, turkeys or poultry from isolated farmsteads. Moorland sheep were also very vulnerable because they roamed freely on the open heights, often providing a simple target for a thief armed with a rifle along with the transport necessary to quickly remove the carcass.

Sheep shot like this were often skinned on the spot and then sold within hours to certain urban butchers who asked no questions. The reason for skinning the sheep on the spot was to remove all identification marks—all moorland sheep have coloured dye marks on their fleece. These identify their owners—a sheep with a blue shoulder, for example, would belong to one farmer; one with a red right rump or a red shoulder would belong to others, one with a green flank or blue flank to yet others and so forth. When roaming the wilds of the moorland heights, one owner's sheep would often mingle with another flock, hence the need for a readily visible means of identification.

A closer examination might, in some cases, find the owner's identification mark either burned into a horn or in the form of a personalized ear-clipping. The thieves also ensured these were removed before trying to sell their ill-gotten gains.

Offering crime prevention advice to livestock owners was therefore not easy, and it was rarely accepted. It was quite true that farmers and landowners knew better than the constabulary—for example, suggesting that a lowland farmer locked his field gates to prevent theft of sheep or cattle was never acceptable. A determined thief would simply drive his vehicle into the gate and smash it down or he would cut the lock free with bolt cutters. Such damage was not necessary if the gates were left closed but unlocked—and a locked gate was no deterrent. Besides, a locked gate was something of a hindrance to a busy farmer. Geese were rarely, if ever, stolen because they made such a racket when disturbed (which is why geese roam free around many farmstead—they make good watchmen), but thieves could steal poultry from hen-houses under cover of darkness when the birds would not raise much noise. To keep a hen calm and silent you simply cover its head with a bag or sack.

Horses were also subjected to theft, even from racing stables, although I must admit I never came across a case of pigs being stolen on my patch, probably because they can make far too much noise when disturbed. It dawned on most rural police officers that the landowners and farmers themselves are best at preventing the specialized crimes with which they are targeted. Down the centuries and even into modern times, many have formed self-help associations to protect their interests, often with night patrols and now with constant contact through mobile telephones. On occasions, these associations might provide a tip-off to the police, and so a joint operation could be mounted, often with considerable success.

In spite of their skill at preventing or minimizing crimes relating to their livestock, it was often noticed by police officers that farmers and the occupants of large country houses were not quite so clever or organized at protecting their domestic belongings. Country houses, widely regarded as homes of the wealthy, have long been a target for burglars and thieves, hence the protective high walls and gates which often surround them. But while such walls might prevent easy access to the premises, the houses themselves were often very vulnerable, having lots of ground-floor windows, doors, disused rooms and cellars. It was quite easy, too, to gain access to the spacious roofs and enter through lofts and attics. It meant that breaking into such a house, or even using an unlocked door or window to gain entry, was frequently very simple.

The snag was, and perhaps still is, that when a burglar breaks into such a large house, his presence may not be heard by the occupants, even when they are in residence. For example, I know of one house, only moderately sized in comparison with some, whose drawing-room was demolished by a runaway lorry while the family was having breakfast at the other end of the house. And they never heard a thing.

Today, with sophisticated alarm systems and more efficiently secured windows and doors, our splendid country houses are well protected against the rogue members of our increasingly lawless society—although those which are open to the public (as so many are) still suffer thefts, even while attendants are patrolling vulnerable rooms. In one country mansion near me, a valuable ornamental lampshade disappeared from a light hanging in the middle of the room—and it was removed during opening hours with attendants and visitors nearby.

With several historic country houses on my Aidensfield beat, I was in regular touch with their owners and, in general, was satisfied with their crime prevention techniques. Security of their ancestral home and its contents was considered essential; they have survived many assaults in the past, both legal and illegal, and will continue to do so.

However, it was a vastly different matter so far as some of the farmers and village people on my patch were concerned. One might argue that they were far too trusting with their homes and contents while others might suggest they were somewhat careless.

In this respect, one area of concern to me, even in the 1960s, was that few farmers and country folk bothered to keep their money in banks. They kept it in the house, in what they thought was a safe hiding place, but in the eyes of professional thieves, there is no such thing as a safe hiding place. If the money is hidden in a house or outbuilding, they will find it. That is how they live.

Those lovely, trusting village people did not bother with banks because they, the people, dealt in cash. They were paid their wages in cash and bought all their requirements with cash. Consequently they saw absolutely no reason to worry about banks and obscure things like cheque books, interest rates, deposit accounts and current accounts. If they saved anything and wanted it treated in an official way, they put their cash into a Post Office Savings Account or National Savings; if not, they kept it somewhere in the house. One benefit with the post office was that there was a branch in most rural communities, however small they were, and this avoided the need to go traipsing into town each time money was needed, or deposits were to be made.

Quite often, I would find housewives with special tins, all marked, and all containing money. They were usually positioned around the kitchen or sitting-room. One tin would be for the butcher, one for the grocer, one for the insurance man, another for savings to buy a new dress or pair of shoes, another for petrol and another for taxing and insuring the car or tractor and yet another for the Sunday collection in church.

There was always one for Christmas, into which was placed a regular amount of cash each week throughout the year, and sometimes a similar one for family birthdays. Such money was always available—it was never placed in a bank.

As I chatted to some of the older people during my rounds I realized a high percentage of them utterly failed to understand the system of banking. When I asked one old character, who was a highly successful cattle dealer as well as a busy farmer, and whom I knew had just completed a deal worth £20,000, why he did not use a bank, he said, 'I don't want my money being stolen.'

'How do you mean?' I pressed him.

'Well,' he said, 'if robbers break in, or hold up the manager with a gun, they'll get away with my cash!'

'Well,' I tried to explain, 'It wouldn't actually be your cash.'

'Whose would it be then? If I put twenty-thousand into Barclays Bank in Ashfordly, and some thief comes in with a gun and steals twenty-thousand, it must be my cash!'

'No, it would belong to the bank,' I tried to explain.

'Nay, lad. It would be mine. Nobody else hereabouts does deals like me, not for that sort of money. And I don't want to lose my hard-earned cash to some thief, Mr Rhea; I need it handy when I'm doing my deals.'

'You mean you keep it here, in the house?'

'Aye, I've allus done that. Allus dealt in cash, Mr Rhea. I never take cheques; you can't trust em. Just a bit o' paper—I like to see my money! Cash on the nail, that's me.'

I was speaking to him in my crime prevention capacity, trying to persuade him to open a bank account because I knew he kept a lot of money in the house. I thought he was very vulnerable—and if I thought like that, others must also know that he kept a lot of money at home, as indeed most of his customers did. Word of his hidden hoard could easily reach the ears of crooks. I did not know where in the house he concealed his wealth but, judging by the deals he brokered, I knew he must have substantial amounts hidden around the place. However, I did try to explain how the banking system operated, stressing that he was in no danger of losing his money if the bank was raided, but he could not understand my logic. I think he saw local banks as places where people put boxes of cash with their names on, to be available whenever required. I tried to suggest his money was in greater danger of being stolen from his own house but he said, 'Nay, lad, I've hidden it well.'

He was not the only character to conceal money in his premises—I learned of an itinerant traveller who dealt in horses and scrap iron, and he kept more than £200,000 in cash in his caravan! He kept it there so that the taxman would never get his hands on it and used some of it to buy parcels of land, always for cash. Similarly, I knew of a racehorse trainer who never went anywhere with less than £25,000 cash upon him.

In all cases, these characters did not understand or trust the banking systems—and, I suspect, they were also keen on keeping their money away from the clutches of the tax man.

In trying to make them understand our monetary system, I recall one story of a farmer and his wife from the North York Moors who kept their savings in a milk churn in the pantry. That was where surplus cash was 'put by' at the end of each week. The churn was full of bank notes, those at the bottom turning green with mould. Eventually, the couple were persuaded to open an account and deposit their savings in a bank. They contacted a local manager by telephone and arranged to bring in the money one Wednesday morning.

'How much will there be?' asked the manager.

'Five thousand pounds,' said the farmer.

'Five thousand?'

'Aye, it's money we've been putting by.'

At the time, £5,000 was around ten times the annual wage of a professional person, and so this was a huge amount, especially by local banking standards. On the due date, therefore, the farmer's wife loaded the milk churn full of notes onto the back of their tractor and trailer, and off they went to the bank. The manager, knowing what to expect, had arranged for a team of tellers to count the money as quickly and as accurately as possible so that the transaction could be swiftly completed.

At the appointed time, therefore, man and wife carried the churn into the bank and were ushered, with due ceremony, into the manager's sumptuous office. As he began to record their details while explaining the choices available to them, the counting started. It was agreed the couple would have a joint current account plus a deposit account that would earn them some useful sums in interest. They were advised how to make good use of both accounts without becoming overdrawn. Then the bad news came.

'There isn't five thousand pounds in this churn,' said the senior teller.

'Isn't there? So how much is there in it?' asked the farmer.

'Four thousand, nine hundred and ninety-five pounds. You're a fiver short.'

'By gum, we've brought t' wrong churn!' said the farmer.

Perhaps the most curious example of how some folk can misunderstand the formalities of banking and money, and also the intricacies of legal matters such as wills and inheritance, came to me on a Thursday morning. It was a phone call from a lowland farmer called Norman Buckle who lived at Swang Farm, Thackerston. Unlike the hill farms, Swang Farm was spread across the floor of the valley with flat fields, a few copses of trees and a pleasant stream trickling through the meadows. It was a very picturesque location which avoided the harsh ruggedness of the higher moorland farms.

The word 'swang' means a low, wet or marshy tract of ground, and in some places the term remains even though the land has been drained and is now dry.

'Now then, Mr Rhea,' he began. 'Buckle here. Will you be coming to Thackerston in t' near future?'

'I can come any time you like, Mr Buckle.'

'Oh, right, well. Call in when you're passing. I'd like a word.'

'OK, no problem. How about half past ten this morning?'

'Champion, it's 'lowance time so t'kettle will be on.'

'I'll be there. Is it something special? Do I need to do some research before I see you? Some legal thing or problem you want sorting out?'

'Nay, nowt like that, Mr Rhea. Just a bit of advice on looking after some sheep.'

'Sheep?'

'Aye, very valuable sheep. I want to make sure they're protected against thieves and such, and I saw an advert in t'paper, summat about getting free crime prevention advice from t'police. So I thought I'd have words.'

'Right, I'll see you in a short while and we'll see what we can do.'

I must admit I was baffled by this. I knew nothing about caring for sheep but guessed he was seeking some kind of advice on preventing them from being stolen, particularly if they were valuable.

Lowland farmers did not make use of the same system as their colleagues on the moors; in other words, they did not use the coloured fleece system to identify their animals because here in the lowlands, the sheep were all contained in fields with secure hedges or fences. They did not mingle with the flocks of other farmers, consequently such a ready means of identification was not necessary.

At the appointed time, I drove along the twisting unmade road which led through the fields to Swang Farm. Norman Buckle was one of the old type of farmer, probably well into his late sixties or early seventies, but still working on his mixed arable and livestock farm. Wherever he went, he always wore a brown flat cap and slate-blue overalls, so I have no idea whether he was bald or had a good head of hair, except that grey patches showed beneath his cap. But I'd never seen him without his cap, even indoors.

When I arrived, he was occupying himself in the yard by washing his tractor with a hose pipe and yard brush but as soon as he noticed my van, he turned off the water and signalled for me to follow him indoors. Inside the spacious and warm kitchen, a large fire was blazing and the table bore a plate of scones, a pot of jam, a saucer of homemade butter and a large plate of fruit cake. Mrs Buckle—Edna—bade me sit down as she returned the already hot kettle to the fire to make the tea. Norman washed his hands and joined me. His wife disappeared upstairs to allow us to talk in private—she said she had some work waiting in the bedrooms.

As usual, we chatted about the weather, local gossip and the price of farm commodities such as bacon, mutton, wheat and potatoes, and then he turned to the matter of our meeting.

'You'd see my sheep on the way here, Mr Rhea?'

'I can't say I noticed,' I had to admit, adding, 'I wasn't really looking and besides, I hardly know one breed from another. Except blackfaces, of course, I'm used to seeing those on the moors.'

'Aye, well, mebbe they've gone into that dip, I've got 'em in my ten acre, Mr Rhea. It dips down to the beck, so I reckon they'll be down there. Not that they like wet ground, they like to be dry.'

'So if they're a valuable breed, Mr Buckle, what sort are they?'

'Suffolks,' he said.

'Suffolks? That's not a rare breed, is it?'

'Nay, not by a long chalk. You get lots of Suffolks on lowland farms, they look a bit like them blackfaces you get on our moors, but the ewes don't have horns.'

'So now many have you?'

'Fifty-one,' he said. 'All ewes, bar one tup. He can cope with all them.'

I was puzzled now. I knew that some farmers were keen on keeping rare breeds of cattle, sheep or pigs but Suffolks were not a rare breed of sheep—far from it. They were plentiful throughout Britain. So had these sheep been prize winners at important shows?

'Have they won prizes at the Great Yorkshire Show or somewhere?' was my next question.

'No, nowt like that, Mr Rhea. It's just a fairly ordinary small flock of Suffolks; they used to belong to my uncle. Uncle Dick—he died last month. Ninety-four he was. He left these sheep to me, that's how I've come by them.'

'Clearly, they mean a lot to you, being owned by your uncle?'

'Not really,' he said. 'There's nowt special about those sheep . . . well, there wasn't until Uncle Dick died.'

'So now they're valuable?'

'Oh aye, they're worth a fortune, Mr Rhea. Which is why I'm asking for your advice.'

'I think you'll have to explain why they're so valuable, Mr Buckle, because I don't understand. If they're not special in any way, not a rare breed and not prize winners, how can they be valuable?'

'Uncle Dick left a lot of money for them,' he said. 'In his will.'

'He's willed money to the sheep?'

'Aye,' he said. 'Like some folks leave money for pet cats and dogs, he's left his to those sheep.'

'So if it's not a rude question, how much as he left them?'

'Well, he had a very big spread down south, a gentleman farmer he was, so the cash he's left meant them sheep are worth nearly five hundred apiece,' he said. 'Twenty-five thousand pounds, he left 'em.'

'That's a lot of money!'

'Aye, it is. But he was very well off, he was a good businessman and did a bit of trading on the stock market. So you can see my problem.'

'Go on, tell me more.'

'Well, you can buy a good sheep at market for summat like fifteen quid, it makes these very expensive animals, Mr Rhea. Each of 'em is worth a fortune . . . so you can see why I need your advice. How can I make sure they don't get stolen? Or shot in the fields. Or whatever else can happen to valuable animals.'

'Mr Buckle, those sheep aren't any more valuable because your uncle has left them money. They're still the same sheep . . . presumably he's left the money so they'll be cared for? Which is why some people leave money for their cats and dogs, to guarantee their welfare.'

'Well, I'm not sure about that. All I know is that when I got that letter from his solicitor, it said Uncle Dick had left twenty-five thousand pounds for the sheep, and I was to get them so I could look after them. That's why they're here, in my field.'

'That might be so but it doesn't make each sheep worth any more,' I tried to explain. 'If someone came here one night and stole those sheep, they'd only be worth their current market value, not an extra five hundred pounds each.'

'Aye, but if Uncle Dick left money for the sheep, then somebody might nick 'em to get their hands on that money. I mean, if they took all Uncle Dick's sheep, surely they'd do it to get their hands on that money. Like folks steal valuable paintings or silver, to sell it and get the money, just like they might steal a prize bull or a top racehorse.'

'It doesn't work like that.' I realized I was having difficulty in getting through to him. He had his mind firmly set on believing that each sheep was worth a fortune and I wondered how I could persuade him otherwise. Then I asked, 'Have you a copy of the will? The bit that mentions the sheep might help us decide what Uncle Dick really meant.'

'Aye, it's in my bureau.' He left the table and disappeared into his office at the back of the house, then returned with a file. In it was a copy of the last will and testament of Mr Richard J. Buckle, a resident of Shropshire. He found the relevant section and placed it before me. Although couched in legal jargon, I could understand it. It said, *To my nephew, Norman Stanley Buckle of Swang Farm, Thackerston in the North Riding of Yorkshire, I leave my flock of Suffolks with twenty-five thousand pounds*. And that was all it said.

Now I could see a problem. I would have thought Uncle Dick meant the £25,000 was for his nephew, not the sheep, but the wording was not quite clear. I did not feel qualified or suited to determine the matter and so I asked, 'Have you spoken to Uncle Dick's solicitor about this? I think it needs a bit of clarification.'

'Nay,' he admitted. 'I just got a letter with a copy of his will, and a note saying the sheep would arrive within a day or two, and the money would follow when Uncle Dick's estate has been settled. That means selling the farm and house and so on. I haven't got the money yet, just them sheep.'

'I didn't read the other clauses, Mr Buckle, but has your uncle left anyone else money like that?'

'Aye, my brother. He lives in Wales. He got my uncle's horses, three beauties, and twenty-five thousand—'

'For himself or the horses?' I interrupted.

'Nay, I don't know. That's how it sets it out it in the will—all Uncle Dick's horses with twenty-five thousand pounds.'

'Have you spoken to your brother?'

'Nay, we've not spoken for twenty-five years, not since he ran off with the milkman's daughter. And him a married man. We don't like that sort of thing in our family.'

'Then I think you should have a chat with your uncle's solicitor, to see if he can help interpret that clause, or both clauses. I'd say he's left the money and the flock of sheep to you I don't honestly think he would want the sheep to have all that money!'

'You mean that money might be for me?'

'That's how I understand it, yes.'

'Well, I'll be blowed. I've never been left anything in my life, never won a raffle prize even. Why would he want to leave me all that money?'

'Probably because you and your brother are his only blood relations, or because he thinks you'll make good use of it, or because he trusts you to do the right thing by him, and his sheep. I don't know . . . but if it's in his will, then that's what he wants. All you have to do, to satisfy your own curiosity, is to give his solicitor a ring.'

'I'm all of a tremble, Mr Rhea. Damn it, I've worked hard all my life to keep my head above water and now this . . . I think I need a glass of whisky before I ring that chap.'

He strode through to the adjoining room, the sitting-room or best room as he would describe it, and I heard the clink of bottle against glass, then he returned with two large measures of Scotch.

'You'd better have one an' all,' he said, plonking a glass before me.

He sipped long and deep as I picked at mine, wondering whether I should imbibe when on duty (this was before the days of the breathalyser), and I knew he wouldn't be offended if I left a few drams.

'By gum, I needed that,' he said eventually. 'It's steadied my nerves . . . now, where's that chap's number?'

He found the solicitor's headed paper with his telephone number and asked the operator to connect him—but then he passed the phone to me.

'You'd best talk to him, Mr Rhea, you understand things better than me. His name's Lee.'

And before I could raise an objection, I heard a woman answer by saying, 'Lee and Stanford, Solicitors. Can I help?'

'Can I speak to Mr Lee please, it's on behalf of a Mr Buckle of Thackerston in the North Riding.'

'And who is calling?'

'I am PC Rhea, the local constable. I am with Mr Buckle now.'

'Just a moment, Mr Rhea, I will see if Mr Lee is free.'

'Francis Lee speaking,' said a voice after a short pause. 'How can I help you, PC Rhea.'

'I am with Mr Buckle now, Mr Lee, at his home in Thackerston. You might recall the case—he has been left a flock of sheep by an uncle in his will . . .'

'I remember it well, Mr Rhea. I trust there is not a problem?'

'It's the wording of the clause which leaves the money. Mr Buckle felt the money was intended for the flock of sheep, Mr Lee, not for him personally. He thought the sheep were all very rich animals . . . now, I've looked at the wording and it is rather obscure . . .'

'It is oddly phrased, I agree, Mr Rhea, but the money is for Mr Buckle, once we get the estate finalized of course. His uncle discussed this with me when he drafted his will. You can assure him of that. I must admit I tried, without success, to get the old man to make the wording more clear, but he wouldn't hear of it.'

'I think Mr Buckle might want a letter of confirmation from you, once things have been completed,' I suggested.

'A good idea, Mr Rhea. Yes, rest assured I will clarify the matter so that any misunderstandings are removed. Tell him to expect something in about four or five months' time.'

And so I passed the good news to Norman Buckle who said, 'I think I'd better have another whisky, Mr Rhea. Then I've got another problem to sort out.'

'Oh, and what's that?'

'It's my missus,' he frowned. 'She's been harping on about a new carpet for our best room . . . I might have to give in to her now.'

* * *

Another ongoing and very widespread problem involved the security of money earned by small businesses that dealt mainly in cash. This was not restricted to the Ashfordly/Aidensfield locality, but was a national worry. The businesses in question included public houses, small shops, cafés and a wide range of similarly modest enterprises, often involving self-employed people. They were not alone in raising police concerns, however; some bigger enterprises also took large amounts of cash from customers and these might include department stores, hotels and even supermarkets which were then making their presence felt across the nation.

At times, it meant substantial amounts of cash were kept on their premises, often in a very insecure manner although strong safes were recommended and sometimes installed. The problem thereafter, as perceived by the police, was that these takings had to be paid into a bank—and that meant a trek through the streets or a drive through the countryside by someone while carrying large sums. The standard crime prevention advice was, where possible, to pay in the takings every day, but most concerns tended to pay in their monies on a weekly basis. Many needed some cash on the premises throughout their working day and, of course, where sales occurred during the evening, like hotels, inns, restaurants, fish-and-chip shops and so forth, it could not always be guaranteed they could pay their proceeds into the bank upon closure of the day's trading. In some cases, night safes were installed in the banks for use out-of-hours by such customers, but that entailed a trek to the bank at inconvenient or even dangerous times.

Generally, the accumulated cash included a mixture of cheques, postal orders and cash in the form of notes and coins and it was surprising how many businesses entrusted the task of taking it to the bank to a young woman or man whose role within the organization was one of the least responsible. On many occasions, I've seen young women pottering through the streets carrying a large heavy bag full of money as they head for the bank, always using the same route and always making the journey at the same time of day.

Within police circles, it was always considered amazing that so few of these money-carriers were attacked and robbed. Whenever we encountered employees undertaking that kind of bank-run, we would contact their bosses to suggest they adopted a different route each day and undertook the trip at differing times. Later, increasingly sophisticated bags or cases appeared on the scene, such as those which could be chained to the carrier's wrist and those which smothered an attacker in something like bright red powder, or purple fluid, or set off a loud alarm if an attack occurred. It is true, of course, that attacks did occur in spite of the precautions, but they were surprisingly rare, particularly in and around the North York Moors. Raids, at national level, were more likely to be targeted against the bullion transporters which delivered the banks' own cash into the premises—after all, the loot from such a vehicle could be a massive sum in cash even if the risks were infinitely greater. Those large deliveries were subject to their own powerful security measures, often with specialists in charge of the operations, and if a particularly large transaction was to take place, the local police would be informed in advance.

In a small market town like Ashfordly, and a smaller village like Aidensfield, the local police knew all the traders and were familiar with their routines. Without being specifically requested, one of us would arrange to be visible in uniform when an employee was carrying money to the bank and, in spite of our exhortations to alter their routes and timing, few did that with any degree of success.

The problem with a small community is that there are few alternative routes from business to bank—most of

Ashfordly's banks were clustered around the market square which was also home to most of the town's small businesses. Finding a different route each time was almost impossible, and it was equally difficult when travelling from any of the satellite villages into town. The villages did not have banks and so the rural business people had to drive into town, park and then walk to the bank with their precious load—and there was only one direct road from Aidensfield into Ashfordly, a fact which applied to most of the other villages. As a consequence, it was more by good luck than good management that none of our cash carriers was attacked and robbed. Or it might have had something to do with the fact there was usually a uniformed bobby on duty in Ashfordly market-place when such transactions were being undertaken.

During my time at Aidensfield, I made a point of knowing about all the rural businesses on my patch and nearby, and introducing myself to their proprietors, often with the sole intention of making sure they received practical crime prevention advice. This applied not only to transporting their cash to the bank, but also security of the premises at night and care of the stock during opening hours—shoplifters were at work everywhere. One such business was Orchard Garden Supplies at Elsinby, owned and run by George and Julia Myers. Their spacious house was Orchard House on the tiny lane which twisted and turned through the fields until it reached Ploatby some two miles away.

Orchard House was, therefore, well off the so-called beaten track; it was a spacious old property built of stone and it occupied some five acres of flat and highly fertile land. George, in his mid-fifties, had worked for a company in York but had suddenly found himself redundant when his employers had been taken over by a larger group. George, whose skills lay in marketing, found himself out of a job with a mortgage still running and all the expenses of running and maintaining Orchard House. His wife, Julia, was a trained secretary who worked for a travel agent in Ashfordly, but her modest salary was insufficient to maintain their lifestyle.

They had two sons, but both worked and lived away from home, so they had only themselves to think about.

George tried to find another job, but at his age no one seemed willing to employ him and so, cushioned by his redundancy money, he decided to knock his garden into shape while looking out for suitable work. Both he and Julia had always wanted a lovely easily worked garden full of colourful plants, flowers, a water feature, places to sit quietly and enjoy the sunshine and so, being of a practical nature, he set about transforming part of one of his fields. He worked alone in a very methodical way and soon had one corner looking extremely attractive. His last task was to buy a rustic seat and so he did, placing it on his drive near his front gate while he finished off the site where it would be set.

A passing motor stopped his Land Rover and approached George, asking, 'Is that seat for sale?'

George, knowing he could easily obtain another smiled and said, 'It is, I've just finished it.'

He added a few pounds onto the price he had paid, the man produced the necessary cash, put it in the back of his Land Rover and drove off. George went straight back to the supplier but this time bought two seats—one for his garden and the other for sale. He also bought a pair of bird baths, a rustic arch and a small electric lawnmower—all this he could use if he wished. And, as he worked, he placed them on his drive—and they were sold the following day, a Sunday.

George now realized he had the beginnings of a business—people wanted instant gardens and that included plants—with his fertile spread, he could nurture seeds and sell plants; he could sell garden furniture, tools and equipment. And so Orchard Nurseries began as a fledgling business and by the time I arrived in Aidensfield it was flourishing. Julia had left her job to become company secretary and they employed a couple of local people, one, Fred, as a gardener and the other, a young woman called Sophie, to staff and administer their small shop which sold seeds, plant pots, garden tools, gardening books, bird feeders, lawn mowers, chain saws, concrete blocks, wood of every kind and a host of other things needed for a modern garden. George had a simple philosophy for expansion—every time he sold an item, he replaced it with two, and so his enterprise grew quickly. He sold very high quality goods and his home-grown produce, such as flowers, fruit, vegetables and young plants, was always reliable. I thought he and Julia were a hard-working example to others and whenever I drove along the lane between Elsinby and Ploatby, I would make time to pop in for a chat and a look at his latest lines—and there was usually a cup of tea and a cake!

It was during those visits that I realized his system for paying in the week's takings was far from secure. Because he and Julia were always so busy during their working week, they had no time to drive into Ashfordly—a twenty-minute journey—simply to pay in their money. At the end of each working day the takings were checked and counted, then placed in a safe place inside the house until they were banked. And it was their assistant, Sophie, who took the money to Ashfordly.

Sophie, a young married woman from Elsinby, was totally reliable and had proved herself to be very efficient in staffing the sales office with its simple accounting procedures, stock control and customer care. However, she also cared for her mother who was confined to the house and, during her one-hour lunch break, would drive into Ashfordly on a Friday, market day, to do her mother's shopping, her own shopping and banking—and so George had suggested she take Orchard Nurseries' money at the same time; if she did that, he would allow her to use the company van for the trip. The money was in one of Orchard's own carrier bags and he gave her an extra half-hour on her lunch break. For Sophie it was a wonderful arrangement that helped enormously with her rather frantic domestic routine—and thoughtful gestures of that kind were typical of George.

However, I could see risks in that generous arrangement. Every Friday at 12.15 p.m., Sophie would leave Elsinby in the company van with its Orchard House logo and drive to Ashfordly some six miles away, park in the market-place just after 12.30 p.m. and go about her banking routine, both personal and business. I had no idea how much money she carried each week on behalf of Orchard Nurseries but it would be substantial and probably into several thousands of pounds. That kind of money would be vital for the continuing cash-flow of the business—to have it stolen would be catastrophic.

When I carried out a subtle questioning of Sophie over tea one afternoon, I discovered that paying Orchard's money into the bank was the first thing she did upon arrival in Ashfordly each Friday. She wanted rid of the money—which was in cheques, notes and coins carried in a bag with the company name on it—rather than leave it unattended in the parked van. It meant, of course, that she was now rather vulnerable because she had slipped into a routine—doing the same task at the same time every Friday in a very recognizable vehicle—but with several thousand pounds in her care. Both she and the money must be at risk. In this part of England, the risk was low, but it could not be ignored.

As I pondered the best way of approaching George about it, the Home Office announced one of its drives to raise the nation's awareness of the need for crime prevention and so, the next time I popped into Orchard Nurseries, I was armed with a pile of leaflets.

As we enjoyed our customary tea, I raised the matter of Sophie's regular trip to the bank. George, Julia and Sophie listened patiently as I waffled on with my crime prevention patter, and nodded as I steered the discussion towards Orchard Nurseries and their banking procedures. I expressed concern that Sophie was following a very identifiable routine every Friday while carrying what was obviously a large amount of company cash in a named van and named bag. They all listened in silence, sometimes nodding with agreement if I raised a particular point, and after a while I thought I detected knowing smiles on their faces. I began to wonder if I was literally trying to teach granny how to suck eggs—something was amusing them.

When I had finished, I waited for their reaction and George acted as spokesman.

'Well done, Nick,' he beamed. 'It shows you're doing your job with our interests at heart. Good stuff. I'm pleased you've spotted Sophie's trips—if you've noticed them, then it's likely a thief might have done the same, just as you say. It's something we're always aware of.'

'So Sophie will change her route maybe? And timing? And perhaps use an unmarked car or bag sometimes?'

'No, Nick, she won't—because that bag she carries is empty. There's nowt in it. Sophie's is a dummy run, Nick. If she gets held up, she'll hand the bag over with nowt in it. She does go to the bank to cash her mum's cheque but that's only a few quid.'

'So when do you pay your money in?'

'Any old time,' he said. 'Julia often goes into Ashfordly shopping when thing are quiet in the nursery so she takes it in an unmarked car. She goes at all sorts of different times on different days in different vehicles, sometimes alone and sometimes with friends. Absolutely no routine, Nick, and we always try to avoid having large sums in this house. Sophie's a decoy: she's not bothered about being held up and, if she is, she'll hand over an empty bag. So I give her an extra-long lunch hour for that help. Good crime prevention, eh?'

'Very good,' I said. 'Yes, very good indeed.'

I praised them for their initiative but when I left, I was unsure how to react—was this the kind of tactic I could recommend to other businesses? Or should I stick to the accepted teachings?

I decided to follow an old sergeant's advice—'Deal with every case on its merits, lad,' he had said. 'And don't interfere with other folks' business.'

Nonetheless, Orchard Nurseries' system did have some merit, I thought. And they made a nice cup of tea. Maybe they should start a small tea shop?

CHAPTER EIGHT

Among the routine work of a village constable during my tenure at Aidensfield was an awareness of the old and vulnerable who lived on one's beat. While it is not the professional duty of a police officer to administer to the sick and incapable (there were doctors, district nurses and other experts to do that), it was one of several humane areas which touched the consciousness of all rural bobbies. They did their best to be acquainted with everyone who lived and worked on their patch and, if problems did manifest themselves, the police would inform the relevant authorities or family members. Quite often, there was no one else around to raise the necessary alarm or find help.

That is one of the advantages of village life—although I must stress it wasn't merely the police who did that kind of volunteer duty. Neighbours, friends, family and those whose work involved visiting houses all kept a watchful eye on the vulnerable. Those helpers included people like the postman, priest, vicar and tradesmen who called regularly such as the butcher, fruit and vegetable man, newspaper deliverers, milkman, fish man and so forth. In very general terms, there was usually someone who would set in motion the systems needed to provide the necessary assistance, but at those odd times such as late at night, bank holidays and weekends, that responsibility often fell upon the police. It was something we did instinctively—in simple terms, we kept an eye on what was happening upon our beats.

Pensioners or sick people in whom the police were particularly and understandably interested were former police officers who had either retired or left the force with a sick pension. Another group was police widows. Each police force paid great attention to the welfare of their former colleagues and their families and in the North Riding, there was a procedure by which all pensioners were notified of the death of a former officer or family member. This was done by postcard—but there was a catch! When a police pensioner died, every other pensioner and indeed all serving members of the force, were expected to pay half-a-crown (2s 6d or in decimal terms—twelve and a half pence) as a death contribution. This raised what was, at the time, a considerable sum—something in the region of £90 to £100—which was given to the family of the deceased as a means of helping with the funeral and other expenses in the immediate aftermath of the death. At the time, a police constable's salary was much lower than £1,000 a year, with some long-term pensioners and widows receiving little more than a pittance, and so the input of such a useful sum was wonderful.

Although some pensioners would take their half-crown into their nearest police station, others were either too frail, or lived too far away for that to be a sensible option and so it would be collected by a serving officer. This served two purposes—apart from relieving the pensioner of the responsibility for getting his half-crown to the police station, it generated periodic visits by serving officers which helped in his or her welfare. However, there was another reason for visiting police pensioners. Pensions were paid monthly in advance and this was done by cheque. Pensioners' cheques were delivered by internal private post to the nearest police station so that the nominee could collect the cheque, or alternatively, it could be delivered by a patrolling officer. It meant the authorities did not have to pay postage, but there was a reason for this rather clumsy system: we had to ensure that the person named on the cheque was still alive and qualified to receive it! And so, when delivering the cheque, or if it was collected from a police station, it had to be signed for as proof that the recipient really was the person entitled to receive it, and that he or she was alive. No one questioned this system, probably because it had been in place for years and years.

But things change, as they do. The police authority, along with the County Treasurer's Department, decided that it would simplify matters if the salaries of all county employees and pensioners, including the police, were paid every four weeks instead of once a calendar month. The cheques could be sent by post, although the county authorities asked that recipients consider having their salaries paid directly into their bank accounts. I opted for the latter system—it meant my salary went immediately into my bank account rather than having to wait until I could find time to drive into Ashfordly to pay it in. I thought it was a good system—and so did many others.

But for some, it was a step too far. Typical of the grumbles were those which emanated from Charlie Edwards, a retired police sergeant who lived in Aidensfield.

Visiting Charlie in his rented cottage near the church was one of my regular duties, either to sign the certificate that he was still alive, or to collect his half-crown upon a police death and, of course, I popped in on other occasions merely for a chat and to check discreetly upon his welfare. His wife, Kay, was still alive too, and, with a son and daughter living near Malton, they were a fit and cheerful couple who kept several cats and tended a garden full of flowers. Most of Charlie's service had been as a uniform patrol sergeant in Scarborough and Whitby and it was generally agreed he had been a good sergeant, well able to fulfil his role as a team leader while dealing wisely with the great British public.

Shortly after the salary and pension distribution changes had been implemented, I paid him one of my usual visits. As always, Kay invited me to stay for a cup of tea and a piece of cake because Charlie loved to reminisce about the old days and tell stories of his varied work in those busy seaside towns. On this occasion, however, he did not appear to be in his usual happy and friendly mood.

'I don't like this new pension system,' he grumbled, after we had exchanged pleasantries.

'The four-weekly pay period, you mean?' I tried to clarify his point.

'Aye, Nick, it's all right having my pension paid directly into my bank account—that's a good idea. I don't have to drive into Ashfordly to pay it in—I'm all for that, and the Aidensfield Stores will cash a cheque for me. No, it's because I think we've all been diddled out of money.'

'Diddled out of money? How do you mean, Charlie?'

'Well, it affects serving officers like you as well as us pensioners, so I'm surprised no one's made a fuss about it.'

'I understand our local branch of the Police Federation was in full agreement with the idea and, so far as pensioners were concerned, NARPO gave it the thumbs-up. They represent us all, Charlie; they agreed on our behalf.' NARPO is the National Association of Retired Police Officers, and there is a local branch in every police force. 'And the system is being used for everyone paid from County Hall—fire brigade, teachers, ambulance drivers, clerical staff—the lot. Pensioners included. And all their unions have agreed.'

'That might be so, Nick, but I'm not as daft as some of those who reckon to look after our welfare. They've been conned, Nick, make no mistake about it. We've all been conned.'

'How do you make that out?'

'We've been robbed of a day's pay.'

'I don't think so, Charlie. That would never get past the auditors or anyone else. What gives you that idea?'

'It's like this,' he said. 'Take the old system—I got a pay cheque and then I got a pension cheque at the end of every month. Dated the last day of the month, no matter how many days there were in the month. It even catered for leap years. That's how it used to be. Straightforward.'

'Right,' I said. 'I'm with you so far. And those cheques varied their amounts by just a little every month because of the differing number of days.'

'Exactly,' he beamed. 'That's what I'm leading up to. So now we get paid every four weeks, regularly. Every four weeks like clockwork . . . same amount each time . . . every fourth Friday. Pensioners and serving officers alike. And civilian staff.'

'Right,' I nodded, wondering where his argument was leading. 'Which gives us thirteen pay days a year. Paid directly into our bank accounts, or by a cheque in the post if we prefer.'

'Absolutely right,' he said with a note of triumph. 'So how many days is that? Twenty-eight days multiplied by thirteen—that comes to three hundred and sixty-four by my reckoning.'

'So?'

'So? What do you mean by "so", Nick? There's three hundred and sixty-five days in an ordinary year—three sixty-six in a leap year. So, we're being done out of a day's pay. This year, I get paid for three sixty-four days, not three sixty-five. That's what I'm saying. And when leap year comes round, I'll be robbed of two days' pay.'

For a few moments, I must admit I was puzzled by his logic but then the answer came swiftly.

'No, Charlie. Those thirteen pay days pay you for fifty-two weeks precisely, not a year which is fifty-two weeks and a bit.'

'Exactly what I'm trying to say, Nick. It's the bit that matters.'

'Yes, but the following pay period starts a day early—it doesn't wait for the three hundred and sixty-fifth day to pass by, does it? You get paid on the three hundred and sixty-fourth day and the next pay period starts the following day—day number three sixty-five. Your pay or pension for that day comes at the end of that next four-week block. So you get paid for it.'

'That might be how you see it, but I still reckon I'm being paid one day short of my entitlement.'

'No you're not.' I tried once more to explain. 'In the present system, you are not being paid for a year. You are being paid for three sixty-four days. And the next batch starts immediately after the preceding one. You're not being robbed of a day's pension, Charlie.'

He wasn't convinced.

I could see it was causing him some deep concern so I suggested he wrote to the secretary of NARPO to air his theories. I am sure that when I left him he remained unconvinced by my arguments, and I was later to learn that several police officers and civilian staff had also complained about being short-changed for the same reasons. In this, I was reminded of the words of an old, retired colonel who once said to me, 'Reforms are all right, lad, so long as they don't change anything.' And changing one's method of payment of a salary or pension can be guaranteed to cause something of rumpus.

Later when I called again to see Charlie, he referred to the matter, saying he had written to NARPO as I had suggested, but they had put forward the same reasoning as I.

In spite of their reassurances, he remained stolidly convinced he was being robbed of a day's pay every year—and two days in a leap year.

* * *

One of the youngest pensioners living on my beat had not been a member of the police service, but was a former army commando in the Second World War. I was never sure of his age but his appearance with grey hair and a slight propensity to being overweight suggested he was in his early fifties; he was a handsome man and now ran a successful furniture-making business in Thackerston, one of the villages upon my patch. Just as the police paid regular visits to their pensioners, so personnel from the military welfare section called on this man.

I had few dealings with him—for example, he did not hold either a firearms certificate or a shotgun certificate, both being reasons for regular visits by a local constable. Similarly, he kept no livestock such as pigs or sheep, another reason for the bobby to call and check stock records or to issue movement licences. But whenever I was in Thackerston with a few minutes to spare, I would pop into his workshop for a chat if I thought he was not too busy—it was possible to see into his premises from the village street and he would often wave as I passed by; he always seemed happy to pause a few minutes.

His work involved the construction of furniture like chairs, tables, stools, cupboards, sideboards and other domestic goods, usually on commission. He seemed to earn a good living, and his wife helped with the book-keeping and accounts; he had a nice stone-built house which adjoined his workshop and he ran both a small Ford Anglia for his domestic requirements and a Bedford 30-cwt van for his business.

It seemed he was not a local man, having come to live and work in Thackerston from the West Riding, but he was firmly settled in Thackerston long before I arrived in Aidensfield. His name was Stephen Wintergill and his wife was called Joyce. She would be in her late forties, I estimated, a handsome woman with dark hair who was always very well dressed. So far as I knew they had no children or grandchildren and seemed to be devoted to one another for they seldom socialized, either at village events or by visiting local pubs. As the village people said, 'They keep themselves to themselves'. No one had any complaints about the couple, however; indeed they seemed liked by all and many residents of Thackerston and district would obtain their hand-built furniture from Wintergills, as his business was known.

During the few times I popped in for a social chat, or perhaps to leave some crime prevention literature with him, he never spoke in detail about his life in the army. Although he said he had served during World War II, I had no idea to which regiment he had belonged, or where he had been posted during his service; I did not know his rank either.

I never knew of him attending a reunion of any kind or visits from former colleagues, apart from those in the welfare section, and so, in some ways, Stephen Wintergill was rather a man of mystery. In my frequent visits to other residents of Thackerston, few mentioned Stephen except in the context of his woodworking expertise, and none seemed overtly curious about his exploits in the war. Perhaps he had made it clear he did not wish to speak about his past?

I learned he and his wife had come to Thackerston very soon after the end of World War II, almost immediately after his demobilization which meant he had lived there for some fifteen years or so before my arrival. I estimated he'd be in his early thirties at that time which meant his period in the army was probably restricted to wartime rather than opting for a military career in peacetime.

During the short time I knew him, therefore, I discovered, during an informal chat with a local farmer who knew Stephen very well, that he was prone to what the farmer called 'dark moments'. These were not regular occurrences, but afflicted him from time to time causing him to be off work for a few weeks at a stretch when medical experts, with army experience, came to minister to him. For some reason, his wife always called military doctors and they always came to visit him. I'd heard of some people suffering from serious migraines which sounded a little like the description of Stephen's illness, but I was told it was not migraine—clearly, it was something to do with his wartime experiences.

Whenever he suffered an attack, he overcame it fairly quickly and resumed his life and work as if nothing had happened. And through it all, his wife cared for him without asking anything from the villagers, not even those who were her closest neighbours. It seemed whatever the problem was, they were going to keep it private and indeed, there was no reason to do otherwise because it affected no one except themselves.

It was during a very hot summer while I was serving at Aidensfield that Stephen suffered one of his attacks. It was the first he'd suffered since I became the village constable and I became aware of his incapacity because a handwritten note appeared on his workshop door. It said, *Closed until further notice. Sorry, Stephen Wintergill.* From discreet enquiries I made around the village from those who knew him, it was confirmed he was suffering from those so-called 'dark moments'. His wife, Joyce, continued with her daily routine, fending off all close enquiries about Stephen by saying, 'Give him time; he'll be as right as rain in a week or two; it's not serious.'

It was with some surprise, therefore, that I received a phone call from her a couple of days or so after his workshop was closed.

'PC Rhea, can you call and see Stephen when you've a spare moment or two? He'd like a chat with you.'

'Yes, of course. When would be convenient?'

'Probably one afternoon this week, three o'clock or thereabouts. At the house.'

'All right, how about tomorrow? I have to come to Thackerston on another matter and could easily pop in.'

'Good, thank you. I'll tell him.'

'Can I ask the purpose of his request? I mean, do I need to do any research into a particular law or practice?'

'Oh, no, it's nothing like that. He'll explain when he sees you. And thank you.'

When I arrived at the house, I knocked on the back door as was the custom in moorland villages and Joyce Wintergill responded. With a calm smile, she invited me inside and asked if I would like a cup of tea and a piece of chocolate cake before I went upstairs to see Stephen. I guessed she had a reason for providing me with some advance information about my visit, and so I agreed. She led me through to the comfortable lounge where a log fire was burning and bade me be seated in one of the armchairs.

'You will have heard Stephen isn't well,' she began, after we had discussed the weather and some local gossip.

'I saw the sign on his shop door,' I acknowledged.

'It happens from time to time,' she said. 'It is something he has learned to live with, but he always wants the local policeman to know about his condition, which is why I've called you here.'

'I've not attended him before, like this—'

'No, there's been no need. He's been quite well since you came to Aidensfield, but now he's having one of his dark moments—that's his name for it, Mr Rhea. Some of our neighbours who know him well use it too—to describe or explain his illness. Most think it's migraine, but it's not.'

'But from what you said on the phone, he's well enough to talk to me?'

'Yes, he prefers to tell you himself, rather than have me explain on his behalf. He thinks it does him good, to talk to someone other than me or his doctors.'

'A policeman seems an odd choice,' I heard myself say.

'You will see how sensible it is when you've heard what he has to say, Mr Rhea. I'll take you up in a minute or two—his bedroom is all in darkness, with black blinds and heavy curtains, but there's a low light burning. He's had his cup of tea. I took it up just before you arrived and so I'll go and see if he's ready for you. You sit and finish your tea—I might be a few minutes; I need to be sure he's ready.'

As I sat and pondered the curious situation, she disappeared and I heard her climbing the stairs somewhere nearby and then footsteps across the floor above my head. I did not hear any of their conversation but after a lapse of some five minutes, I heard the footsteps again. She was coming downstairs. She appeared, smiling and relaxed. 'Stephen will see you now, Mr Rhea.'

I followed her upstairs and she led me into the darkened bedroom where a nightlight burned beside the bed. He was propped up with pillows and leaned against the headboard, a pale figure in the gloom. In spite of the room being in darkness, sufficient daylight was filtering through the curtains and blind for me to see moderately well within the room, even if some areas were in deep shadow. There was a chair beside the bed and so I settled upon it as Joyce left us alone.

'You'll be wondering what this is all about, Mr Rhea?'

'I must admit I am rather puzzled—it's not often a village bobby visits the sick in this way. I feel rather like a priest coming to hear your confession! And you can call me Nick—most people do.'

'And I'm Stephen—I know we've often had nice chats in my workshop, but we've never been properly introduced,' and he extended his hand for me to shake. I did so. He chuckled as he added, 'So, it's time to make my confession! That's more apt than you realize.'

He paused before continuing and I must admit I wondered if he was going to admit committing some serious crime in the past, but I waited until he felt he could continue.

'I was a commando during the war,' he began. 'I didn't volunteer—I was selected for that specialist work. It seems that, quite unwittingly, I passed some aptitude tests which were imposed upon us without us realizing and because of that, I was selected for special training.'

'Sounds just like the army to me!' I smiled. 'Never volunteer!'

'Right; it was typical. I was very young and very fit then—I played football, cricket, rugby, did cross-country racing, judo, high jumping—I was good at all sports, Nick.'

'A good training ground for a commando, I would think.'

'Yes. One thing it taught me was to think on my feet and react immediately—and instinctively—to situations. You learn how to avoid having your legs kicked from under you by unscrupulous opposing players; you learn how to dodge cricket balls aimed at your head . . . you know what I'm saying?'

'Yes, I know how important sports of all kinds are in military training.'

'Yes, dealing effectively with swiftly moving situations on the sports field helped commandos to deal just as swiftly with situations in wartime—I'm talking about close combat here, Nick, life-threatening close combat. Hand-to-hand fighting, not sitting with a target yards away at the end of your rifle barrel. Literally hand-to-hand, instant reaction stuff; life or death situations—fighting without a weapon . . . I can break a man's arm, his neck even, bare-handed . . .'

His voice trailed away as he spoke and I didn't know whether to interrupt with some acknowledge, or simply allow him to rest awhile. I chose the latter and watched him take several deep breaths before continuing.

'We were sent to Burma. It was in 1944 when Burma was over-run by the Japs. We—the British that is—were trying to reverse the situation and I was in a patrol working in the jungle, taking out small Japanese units. By stealth. We slept rough; we stole to eat; we were like animals.'

He paused again and I waited. 'We were killers, Nick. Our job was to destroy the enemy, not to take chances, to be positive . . . and when we slept at night, in the jungle, we were taught to respond immediately if we were threatened. The Japs knew we were there and they tried to creep up on us at night so we had to be silent, no fires, no talking, no noise . . . like snakes in the grass, creeping up on our targets and executing them without a sound.'

Another pause.

'I was taught to kill, Nick. We all were. If a Jap found me asleep, his presence—not his voice, not any noise, rustling of clothes or breathing but merely his presence—was enough to wake me. My job was to reach out and throttle him before he could harm me—remember he had to get close enough to kill me by hand, without a sound, without waking my colleagues. They were doing what we were doing and like us, they had knives. But even knives can make a noise—or the result of using them can make a noise. We killed by hand, Nick, and so did they. And so, if I was disturbed in my sleep, I would wake in an instant and immediately grab the nearest person by the throat and strangle them. I had to—it was either me or him.'

Another pause.

'So why am I telling you this? It's to do with these dark moments that recur from time to time. When I'm asleep during one of those moments, I'm back in Burma, Nick, waiting for a Jap to approach me . . . and if he does, I react instinctively.'

'In a bad dream, you mean?'

'No, in real life. I respond in real life. I will strangle the first thing I get my hands on, the first creature within my reach. Which is why Joyce sleeps in a separate room—and why that huge stuffed teddy bear is beside my bed.'

I hadn't noticed the bear until he pointed it out. It was lying in the shadows on the floor at his side of the bed, a heavy teddy bear about four foot six inches tall, the size of a small child. Or a Japanese soldier?

'He's been strangled more times than I care to admit,' he smiled. 'But it takes seconds for me to adjust to normality . . . but if that was a real person, Nick, it would be too late.'

'Joyce, you mean?'

'Yes. She knows about all this . . . I'm perfectly all right and quite safe until these dark moments arrive. Joyce recognizes the symptoms, then calls in my specialist military doctors, psychologists and counsellors . . . I will grow out of it. We have to use military medical experts due to the sensitive nature of some of the stuff I might shout out . . . state secrets, and all that.'

'Even after all this time? The war's been over for a decade!'

'Sensitivities still exist, Nick. We're bound by all sorts of rules and regulations, both you and me. As I get older, though, my reflexes will slow down and probably when I'm in my dotage, these dreadful experiences will come to an end. I hope so.'

'You say Joyce is not in any danger?'

'I can't guarantee that; I don't want to guarantee that because I could be wrong. I know when these attacks are close and we take the necessary action—she locks herself in her room when I'm asleep, but that's not necessary. I won't walk to launch an attack—I attack from the sleeping position, Nick. I reach out and grab the enemy.'

'At arm's length?'

'Yes.'

'Poor teddy bear!'

'He's had a tough time. Joyce bought him for me a long time ago, but it was a good idea. Fancy a grown man having a teddy bear, eh? What would the neighbours think!'

'What indeed! So, Stephen, what you are telling me is that during those attacks—and only during those attacks—you are a very dangerous person?'

'Yes, that's it in a nutshell.'

'OK, I understand. But why tell me? Why not explain to a local doctor or psychiatrist . . . ?'

'Official secrets. You are sworn too, aren't you? Like all police officers. Not to give away national secrets?'

'Yes, of course.'

'So I must continue to be treated by military experts—once I'm dead, of course, none of this matters. But until then, I must obey the rules.'

'So why are you telling me?'

'I am instructed to keep the local police informed of my condition, Nick. Changes in police personnel means I must keep up to date—so now it's your turn to be updated. It's in case I kill someone during one of my attacks—Joyce or anyone else who might be within arm's reach. The authorities should know of my situation and that can only come from the military, not a civilian doctor.'

'What a dreadful situation to be in!'

'I can live with it, but only just. Anyway, you know as well as me, that the civilian police would be called in to deal with the murder—it would not be a job for the military police. That means I need to keep the constabulary informed. I would have to explain why I committed that crime, Nick, because the civilian doctors don't know of my condition. The court must know of my background.'

'I understand; but I'll need a written statement from you, Stephen, my word or a report of this interview would not be sufficient. And, if the truth is known, then such death would not be murder, would it?'

'No it wouldn't. I would hate to be charged with murdering Joyce though . . . I know any charge would be reduced to manslaughter once the truth was known, but you know what's involved. There's a violent death, man strangles wife . . . publicity, an inquest, a trial . . . anyway, Nick, I have prepared my own written statement so that the civilian police are aware of my condition and can take the appropriate action if circumstances demand it.'

He opened the drawer of his bedside cabinet and eased out a buff envelope. Inside were several handwritten foolscap sheets of paper.

'It's not sealed yet so you can read the contents, Nick, just to let you know that my "confession" is just as I've explained now. Take it home, read it and then seal it. Then it must be handed in person to the senior CID officer in your force. I don't want your sergeant or inspector or anyone else reading this—you must hand it to that senior officer. Tell him why—he should have my earlier letters on file—so it doesn't matter if it takes you a week or two to make personal contact.'

I took the envelope. 'Does Joyce know all this?'

'Yes—aren't I lucky to have her? She could have left me; she could have been terrified by all this, but she's stuck by me—even if she sleeps in a different room for some of the time. But we live well; we love each other and I have a good life—apart from these dark moments.'

I stayed with him for a further twenty minutes or so and found him to be a charming man living with an awful personal problem—it was not as if he'd lost his reason on occasions, or went mad—he just woke up and strangled someone! Downstairs I spoke to Joyce and explained what had transpired and she smiled her understanding.

'He will never harm me,' she said with total confidence. 'I'll make sure he doesn't . . . but he's done what he thinks is right. Thank you for talking to him—and do pop in from time to time, I know he'd welcome a chat.'

It would be a couple of weeks later when I was due at force headquarters at Northallerton to have my Mini-van serviced by the force garage staff that I found the opportunity to deliver Stephen's letter personally to the detective chief superintendent. He listened to my story and accepted the envelope.

'I'll destroy the last one from Stephen Wintergill, Nick; we need to be kept up to date with this. I keep thinking he'll get rid of his problem, but it seems to go on and on. Funny old story, if you ask me, but nothing in this job surprises me.'

In the weeks following, Stephen recovered fully and returned to work and I popped in from time to time to talk to him. We never discussed his dark moments, or his war service, and when I left Aidensfield several years later, he was still in Thackerston making his excellent furniture.

And Joyce was still alive and working at his side. He died several years later and is buried in Thackerston churchyard. Joyce outlived him by a few years but today lies at his side—in complete peace.

When he died, I rang the detective chief superintendent at force headquarters.

'Sir,' I announced. 'It's PC Rhea. With reference to that letter I brought you several years ago . . . from Stephen Wintergill, the ex-commando at Thackerston. He's died and I thought his letter should be destroyed now.'

'I've already done so, Nick. But thanks.'

* * *

An author once said to me, 'If you want to find a good story, have a look at the inscriptions on memorial seats and benches, the sort you find dotted around parks or beside footpaths in the countryside. You find them on the moors, mountain-sides, river-banks, in woods, overlooking the beach—anywhere in fact.'

His words were true. Some of the inscriptions are very poignant, perhaps more appropriate for a tombstone than a bench somewhere in the wilds of Britain but the story is not in the bench itself—it concerns the story behind the inscription. I saw one which read, 'Here together always—Belle and me.' There was nothing else. So who was Belle? A woman or a dog? What is the story behind that inscription, or what should we make of the one which reads, 'Walking now in paradise—Jimmy and Alice, 1956.'

There are many more, far too many to include here, but there is one tale from Aidensfield which precedes such an inscription on a bench high on the North York Moors. It involves a lovely old couple called Sarah and Thomas, more popularly known as Sally and Tom. Their surname was Moses, a rather unusual one in the moorland region. Sally died a few months before I arrived in the village and so I never had the pleasure of knowing her or meeting her, but her husband, Tom, continued to live in their little cottage opposite the war memorial.

A fit and competent eighty-two-year-old with two children—a son and a daughter living in York—he looked after himself for most of the time, although neighbours always ensured his washing was done, his bed linen changed and his house cleaned once in a while. They also made sure he ate at least one good meal per day, either by making him a steak and kidney pie, cooking his Sunday lunch or sending treats like cakes or sherry trifles. In return, he would perform little tasks like doing a spot of work in a helper's garden or collecting things from the Aidensfield Stores. His children and grandchildren were regular visitors, especially at weekends and, of course, I kept an eye on him too. I knew he was up and about if I saw smoke coming from his chimney, or a light in the kitchen, or even the back door standing open. He often left the door open, even in the depths of winter—I think it was a throwback to his days as a farm labourer when the rear hall was little more than a depository for dirty boots and filthy clothes.

Because that door opened into a small porch with the kitchen beyond an interior door, it wasn't really considered as part of 'indoors'. There were times I thought such doors were left open to allow the stench of farmyard muck to escape from boots and working clothes, or to provide somewhere for wet dogs and farmyard cats to sleep—animals weren't allowed in houses (except perhaps pet lambs and day-old chickens in the kitchen). The idea of a cat or dog living in the domestic quarters or bedroom was abhorrent to many country people and farmers. Animals lived out-of-doors in stables, sheds, kennels, or wherever they could find a dry place—when I once suggested to an elderly and rather lonely countrywoman that she might consider a cat as a companion/pet, she retorted, 'Not likely! Cats are for the stables.'

Following Sally's death, Tom took to long walks in the countryside around Aidensfield, both on the moors and in the dale. There were lots of pleasant and not-too-demanding routes, ideal for an elderly gentleman who was not in a rush to get anywhere. Many of the walks were circular and passed delightful country inns, so he would make his way there, have lunch and a couple of pints, and then wend his happy way home. In most of those pubs, he was well known to the staff and locals alike and there is no doubt his outings were beneficial to him.

One of his life-long interests was ornithology and so he could wander the lanes and footpaths spotting birds and noting their movements in spring, summer, autumn and winter. He looked out for seasonal delights such as the winter arrival of the fieldfares, redwings or waxwings, or the summer influx of swallows, swifts, house martins, cuckoos and the various warblers. He noted any variations in their times and places of arrival and departure, their nesting times or the dates the young were hatched. Although he was knowledgeable about wild birds, he never considered himself an expert, merely an enthusiastic amateur. It was a hobby and interest he had shared with Sally.

With the passage of time, I realized Tom was following the routes he and Sally had enjoyed together. In fact, like his neighbours and friends, many of the other villagers also realized that, knowing on Saturdays Tom would head for Thackerston, or on Wednesdays he might cross the valley to Elsinby, then a visit to Rannockdale on a Sunday or to Gelderslack either on a Tuesday or Thursday. These outings weren't undertaken absolutely to that schedule, but it was a rough guide to his movements. Most of us knew that when he wasn't at home, he'd venture forth after a hearty breakfast to walk one of those routes, or another of his many favourites, invariably with Sally in mind.

Then one winter's day Tom wasn't at home during the early morning.

At nine o'clock, a neighbour had noticed his curtains were open but there was no smoke coming from his chimney—and worse was the fact his back door was closed. The neighbour had knocked on the back door and front door, but had received no reply; peeping into the cottage she saw no sign of Tom, but noticed his bedroom curtains were open. Her immediate reaction was that he'd gone to stay with either his son or daughter and so, apart from casually mentioning his absence in the Aidensfield Stores later that morning, she took no further action. After all, Tom did go to stay with his family from time to time, but invariably told his neighbours in advance. Because there was no undue concern in anyone's mind, especially with Tom being so hale and hearty, no one checked any further and no one rang his son or daughter in York.

I had driven past the house on my way to a day's duty in Ashfordly that morning and had not noticed anything that unduly concerned me, but it was upon my return visit that I noticed the house in darkness. At that time of year—late November—that was unusual, unless Tom was staying in York. I stopped my van and went to the house, knocking on the front and rear doors, peering through the windows and shouting through the letter box, but there was no sign of Tom. Whenever he went to stay in York, he told me—that was something I encouraged whenever anyone was likely to be away for a while. Tell the police if the house is going to be unoccupied, and they will keep an eye on it—that was the practice at that time. I could see no sign of a fire glowing in the hearth, no sign of pots on the table or in the kitchen sink, no lights anywhere in the building, no break-in—and no sign of Tom lying on the floor or sitting in his favourite armchair.

The problem was what to do next, without being over-zealous on the one hand or too casual on the other. Breaking in to search for him was not an option, not yet anyway—there were some basic checks I could make first. I went home and rang his son and daughter in turn, explaining the situation without trying to alarm them (their numbers were in my records for whenever he was staying with them). But he was not there—and they had no idea where he might be. He'd not said anything to them about going away. I said I would ask around and contact them again if I had any news, negative or positive. They asked if they should come across to Aidensfield and help to search for him, but I felt not at this stage. We had no reason to fear the worst and we had to exhaust all the possibilities—and his children would be better at home where they could be contacted.

Clearly, I had to try and locate him, particularly as it was a cold night, but was he in trouble? Had he gone to stay somewhere and simply forgotten to tell anyone? Should I break in to see if he was lying dead? I felt I needed to know more before I took drastic action, even if it meant working a double shift. Knowing I might be searching or making enquiries late into the night, I had my tea—a five-minute snack—because if I was to be working overtime and late into a winter's night, I needed some sustenance. Telling Mary I might be very late home, I went into the village to begin my enquiries. I talked to Jack and Jill Carver in the Aidensfield Stores, Harry Fletcher the milkman, George Ward at the pub and others who might have heard something of Tom.

What emerged was that Tom had not been seen that day. He had not been into the shop to get his paper; he'd not been seen going along the street on his way to begin one of his walks, and there'd been no sign of him pottering about his house or garden. None of the villagers had been unduly concerned because they knew he sometimes went off to stay with his family in York—and he had been known to forget to tell friends and neighbours of his occasional absences.

As my enquiries intensified with no sightings or knowledge of him, I instituted my own house-to-house enquiries in Aidensfield, knocking on the door of every house that lined the main street. If I learned nothing, I would have to enter his house, hopefully by using a key held by a friend or neighbour, but if not, then I would have to break in. I hoped he wasn't lying dead in bed.

Fortunately, I struck gold. Philip Owen, a retired accountant who lived at the northern end of the village street, had seen Tom the previous morning.

'He was standing at the bus stop,' he told me. 'I was in the garden and saw him—he saw me and waved.'

'Was he carrying anything? Like a shopping bag? Or even a tent?'

'No, but he had his rucksack on his back and was sensibly dressed for walking—proper boots, waterproofs, sweaters, warm hat and so on. And his binoculars were around his neck, Nick. He was clearly going for one of his walks. But no, he didn't have sleeping bag or tent, I'm sure of that.'

'But he was taking the bus?'

'Yes; I don't know where he would be walking to but I got the impression he was taking the bus part of the way.'

'So which bus would he catch?'

'Well, it was about quarter to ten when I saw him, and the Ashfordly bus leaves that stop at five to ten. It's the only one around that time. He was gone the next time I looked, about fifteen minutes later.'

'So unless someone gave him a lift, we can assume he caught that bus—but Ashfordly? Why catch a bus to Ashfordly if he wanted to go for a walk?'

'I can only think there must be walks which start there and go up to the moors or into the higher dale. I must say,

Nick, that it's the first time I've seen him at that bus stop. Most of his walks start here—he does a circular trip to get home each evening after a pub lunch.'

'OK, thanks, Philip. I'll ask at the bus depot—most of the buses finish their circuits about five thirty or six, except the night runs, so I might catch some of the drivers if I'm lucky.'

I raced down to the bus depot in Ashfordly and when I arrived ten minutes later it was clearly still open with rows of buses standing empty after the exertions of the day. There was an office with staff at work and a rest room for the crews, although most of the crews never remained on the premises for longer than necessary at the end of their shifts. The minute they finished, they checked in their takings, had the vehicle examined for damage or necessary maintenance, and then hurried home. But this time I was lucky. As I entered the vast hangar-like building, a uniformed driver was leaving. I stopped him.

'I'm looking for the driver of the Aidensfield to Ashfordly bus, the one that leaves Aidensfield about five to ten—I'm interested in yesterday.'

'You've found him, Constable! It was me. I put my hands up to that one . . . so, what have I done?'

'We're concerned about one of the villagers, an elderly man called Tom Moses. We think he caught that bus yesterday morning.'

'He did. He was my only passenger from Aidensfield. A nice old man. He got a single to Ashfordly.'

'A single?'

'Yes, he said he was going for a walk. He said he didn't often use the bus.'

When I described Tom to the driver, whose name I learned was Jim Waring, there was no doubt we were talking about the same person.

'So he got off at Ashfordly?'

'Yes. He said he wanted to catch the Shelvingby bus—he had ten minutes to spare for that one. It goes from the far side of the market-place. I pointed him in the right direction and off he went.'

'So this man who rarely used buses, caught two in one day. So will the Shelvingby driver be around?'

'No, his last run finished at four thirty-five; he'll have gone home. His name's Stan—Stan Andrews. He lives in a council house, No. 42 on the Ashtree Estate. He's a pal of mine, that's how I know where he lives.'

'Thanks, I'll see if I can catch him.'

'So what's happened to the old man? Moses you said?'

'Tom Moses. We don't know but he's not at home and no one knows where he is. There's a wee bit of concern, so I'm trying to find him.'

'Well, he didn't catch my bus back to Aidensfield, I can tell you that for sure. I was its driver all day yesterday. I'd say it was a long walk from Shelvingby back to Aidensfield, especially for somebody of his age.'

'That's the problem, he didn't get back.'

'Nasty . . . well, you go and see what Stan can tell you. I'll ask around my mates here, most of us'll be mustering tomorrow morning.'

'Thanks, I'll catch up with you tomorrow if I need to.'

Stan Andrews confirmed that Tom had caught the Shelvingby bus the previous morning, boarding it at Ashfordly after buying a single ticket and getting off in the centre of Shelvingby, clad in hiking gear. Shelvingby is high on the moors about seven miles from Ashfordly. But Tom did not catch the bus back from Shelvingby—it seemed he had decided to walk back home. But the walk from Shelvingby to Aidensfield would be almost twelve miles! I decided I should visit Shelvingby immediately to try and find out where he'd gone after leaving the bus.

Shelvingby is a very small community perched on the slopes of a high hill in the midst of the moors. With only a handful of houses, there is one shop which doubles as the post office, and a smart hotel, the Laverock, whose bar functions as the local pub. At this time of the evening, there were few places to ask if Tom Moses had been seen—but again, I struck lucky. Mrs Hollins in the shop said a man answering his description had gone into her shop yesterday morning around eleven o'clock to buy a couple of bars of fruit-and-nut chocolate, an orange and an apple. He'd been alone and told her he was heading for the summit of Laverock Moor on a sentimental journey. She had not seen him since.

He had not explained what his mission entailed, but I knew that Laverock Moor, the highest part of the western section of the North York Moors, was a bleak, windswept and treeless plateau covered with heather, bracken and rocks, and the home of little more than some hardy sheep and grouse. Several footpaths wound their way to the summit from different points on the lower ground and the southern slope overlooked stunning views across upper Ryedale and across the Vale of York. Mrs Hollins had maps for sale in her shop and so we borrowed one from the shelf and tried to ascertain the route Tom might have taken from Shelvingby. There was only one. The others led from places several miles away.

My problem now was whether to arrange a search party, almost certainly involving the moorland search and rescue team, volunteers and police officers, or to make my own preliminary search on that single route.

'How long's it take to get to the summit by that path?' I asked Mrs Hollins.

'An hour at least,' she said. 'Two in bad conditions—but at least there's no fog tonight and the weather's calm.'

'I'll go,' I told her. 'If I get lost, you know where I've gone . . . I'll tell Ashfordly Police over my van radio before I set off, and I can drive it so far up the slope on that green track. That'll save a few minutes. And I've a powerful torch in the van.'

And that was how I found Tom. After leaving the van in a dark, deserted green lane, I climbed up the steep path; it was clearly defined but rugged and rock-strewn as I struggled up the slope, panting in the cool night air. About halfway up the climb, I passed a seat which had been erected there—it bore a plaque saying, 'In loving memory of John and Mary Greenhowe from their friends, 1959' but nothing else. Tom was not on that seat. The climb became steeper as I neared the summit, my torch picking out my route. I began to shout Tom's name, but got no response. When I paused to get my breath back, I could turn and see behind me the wonderful night panorama with a distant glow from the lights of York and a patchwork of fairy lights spreading for miles in the valley below—villages, small towns and even isolated farms provided that unforgettable twinkling scene, occasionally with a well-lit train speeding between London and Edinburgh, or car headlights moving along the network of lanes and main roads.

And, right at the top, my torch picked out the figure of an old man sitting in the shelter of a massive rock. He was facing south with his back leaning against the stone, and he was looking at the view I had just admired, but his eyes were sightless and his head was slumped upon his chest. It was Tom Moses, and he was dead. At first, of course, I did not realize that—I called his name, then reached out to touch him in case he was asleep, but he was stone cold. I checked his pulse. Nothing. He must have been sitting there since sometime yesterday.

Then I saw a note clutched in his hand. It said, 'Tom and Sally, together now.'

I felt a tingle down my spine—to write that, he must have known he was going to die and then I thought about those single bus tickets he had purchased. A one-way trip to be reunited with his wife.

When it was all over—the task of carrying him down from that lonely place, notifying his family, neighbours and friends, the post-mortem, the coroner's enquiry and the funeral—his son came to see me several weeks later when he was clearing Tom's cottage for sale.

'We, the family that is, would like to place a memorial where he was found,' he told me. 'Do I have to get permission from anyone?'

'What sort of memorial?' I asked. 'Are you thinking of one of those nice oak benches with an inscription?'

'No, we were thinking of putting something on that stone where he was found. We thought we would commission a stonemason to carve a memorial in the stone—using the words on that paper you found. "Tom and Sally together now".'

'A lovely idea,' I said. 'I don't think you'd need permission from anyone, but if I were you, I'd have words with the national park authority, just to be sure. There are lots of stones around the moors with various messages on them so there's lots of precedents. Can I ask what prompted this idea?'

'It was when I was clearing his things. I found an entry in his diary. The day he died was the anniversary of the date he proposed to my mother, and that stone was where he did so. She accepted him and he gave her his ring at that very place.'

I found it all very uncanny but within a year, the carved message appeared on that stone. Even today, it is known as the Moses Stone but few know the story that prompted that simple inscription.

THE END

ALSO BY NICHOLAS RHEA

CONSTABLE NICK MYSTERIES

Book 1: CONSTABLE ON THE HILL
Book 2: CONSTABLE ON THE PROWL
Book 3: CONSTABLE AROUND THE VILLAGE
Book 4: CONSTABLE ACROSS THE MOORS
Book 5: CONSTABLE IN THE DALE
Book 6: CONSTABLE BY THE SEA
Book 7: CONSTABLE ALONG THE LANE
Book 8: CONSTABLE THROUGH THE MEADOW
Book 9: CONSTABLE IN DISGUISE
Book 10: CONSTABLE AMONG THE HEATHER
Book 11: CONSTABLE BY THE STREAM
Book 12: CONSTABLE AROUND THE GREEN
Book 13: CONSTABLE BENEATH THE TREES
Book 14: CONSTABLE IN CONTROL
Book 15: CONSTABLE IN THE SHRUBBERY
Book 16: CONSTABLE VERSUS GREENGRASS
Book 17: CONSTABLE ABOUT THE PARISH
Book 18: CONSTABLE AT THE GATE
Book 19: CONSTABLE AT THE DAM
Book 20: CONSTABLE OVER THE STILE
Book 21: CONSTABLE UNDER THE GOOSEBERRY BUSH
Book 22: CONSTABLE IN THE FARMYARD
Book 23: CONSTABLE AROUND THE HOUSES
Book 24: CONSTABLE ALONG THE HIGHWAY
Book 25: CONSTABLE OVER THE BRIDGE
Book 26: CONSTABLE GOES TO MARKET
Book 27: CONSTABLE ALONG THE RIVERBANK
Book 28: CONSTABLE IN THE WILDERNESS
Book 29: CONSTABLE AROUND THE PARK
Book 30: CONSTABLE ALONG THE TRAIL

Book 31: CONSTABLE IN THE COUNTRY
Book 32: CONSTABLE ON THE COAST
Book 33: CONSTABLE ON VIEW
Book 34: CONSTABLE BEATS THE BOUNDS
Book 35: CONSTABLE AT THE FAIR
Book 36: CONSTABLE OVER THE HILL
Book 37: CONSTABLE ON TRIAL

Thank you for reading this book.

If you enjoyed it please leave feedback on Amazon or Goodreads, and if there is anything we missed or you have a question about, then please get in touch. We appreciate you choosing our book.

Founded in 2014 in Shoreditch, London, we at Joffe Books pride ourselves on our history of innovative publishing. We were thrilled to be shortlisted for Independent Publisher of the Year at the British Book Awards.

www.joffebooks.com

We're very grateful to eagle-eyed readers who take the time to contact us. Please send any errors you find to corrections@joffebooks.com. We'll get them fixed ASAP.

Printed in Great Britain
by Amazon

19502661R00103